Come Back, Little Sheba

A DRAMA IN TWO ACTS

by William Inge

SAMUEL FRENCH

25 WEST 45TH ST.   NEW YORK 19

7623 SUNSET BLVD. HOLLYWOOD 46

LONDON   TORONTO

COME BACK, LITTLE SHEBA

STORY OF THE PLAY

(8 Males; 3 Females)

Come Back, Little Sheba is a play based on a deadly parallel. It has to do with a chiropractor who had to quit medical school and marry the gal. The constant realization of what he might have been rankles to the extent of driving him into occasional binges and the arms of Alcoholics Anonymous.

To make ends meet, his frowsy but loving wife takes in a boarder, a girl student with a midwestern college. When hubby sees her playing fast and loose with a dumb athlete, forgetting a trustful fiance, he takes to the bottle again. But the twist is that the gal, after her fling, marries the right guy.

So the chiropractor, after a siege in a hospital alcoholic ward, comes repentantly back home to resume his hapless life with the only thing he has left to turn to— the ineffectual wife who had knocked all the ambition out of him.

The wife, who has been living in the past, who has been calling to Little Sheba, a lost puppy, finally decides to begin living in the present and future.

Produced February 15, 1950, at the Booth Theatre.

THE THEATRE GUILD

presents

COME BACK, LITTLE SHEBA

A New Play by
WILLIAM INGE

with Shirley Booth, Sidney Blackmer, Joan Lorring

Directed by Daniel Mann

Setting and Lighting designed by Howard Bay

Costumes by Lucille Little

Production under the supervision of
Lawrence Langner and Theresa Helburn

Associate Producer, Phyllis Anderson

CAST

(In order of appearance)

Doc .... *Sidney Blackmer*
MARIE .... *Joan Lorring*
LOLA .... *Shirley Booth*
TURK .... *Lonny Chapman*
POSTMAN .... *Daniel Reed*
MRS. COFFMAN .... *Olga Fabian*
MILKMAN .... *John Randolph*
MESSENGER .... *Arnold Schulman*
BRUCE .... *Robert Cunningham*
ED ANDERSON .... *Wilson Brooks*
ELMO HUSTON .... *Paul Krauss*

4

THE SCENE

An old house in a run-down neighborhood of a Midwestern city.

ACT ONE

SCENE 1: *Morning in late spring.*
SCENE 2: *The same evening, after supper.*

ACT TWO

SCENE 1: *The following morning.*
SCENE 2: *Late afternoon the same day.*
SCENE 3: *5:30 the next morning.*
SCENE 4: *Morning, a week later.*

Come Back, Little Sheba

ACT ONE

SCENE I

*It is the downstairs of an old house in one of those
semi-respectable neighborhoods in a Midwestern
city. The stage is divided into two rooms, the living room at Right and the kitchen at Left, with a
stairway and a door between. At the foot of the
stairway is a small table with a telephone on it.
The time is about 8:00 A.M., a morning in the
late spring.*

*At rise of Curtain the sun hasn't come out in full force
and outside the atmosphere is a little grey. The
house is extremely cluttered and even dirty. The
living room somehow manages to convey the atmosphere of the twenties, decorated with cheap
pretense at niceness and respectability. The general
effect is one of fussy awkwardness. The furniture
is all heavy and rounded-looking, the chairs and
davenport being covered with a shiny mohair. The
davenport is littered and there are lace antimacas-
sars on all the chairs. In such areas, houses are so
close together, they hide each other from the sun-
light. What sun could come through the window,
at Right, is dimmed by the smoky glass curtains.
In the kitchen there is a table Center. On it are
piled dirty dishes from supper the night before.
Woodwork in the kitchen is dark and grimy. No*

6

*industry whatsoever has been spent in making it
one of those white, cheerful rooms that we commonly think kitchens should be. There is no action
on stage for several seconds.*

*Doc comes downstairs to kitchen. Coat on back
of chair Center. Straightens chair. Takes roll from
bag on drainboard. Folds bag, tucks behind sink.
Lights stove. To table, fills dishpan there and takes
it to sink. Turns on water. Tucks towel in vest for
apron. To Center chair, says prayer. To stove, takes
fry pan to sink. Turns on water.*

*MARIE, a young girl of 18 or 19 who rooms in
the house, comes out of her bedroom (next to the
living room), skipping airily into the kitchen. Her
hair is piled in curls on top of her head and she
wears a sheer dainty negligee and smart, feathery
mules on her feet. She has the cheerfulness only
youth can feel in the morning.*

MARIE. *(To chair Right, opens pocketbook there)*
Hi!

Doc. Well, well, how is our star boarder this morning?

MARIE. Fine.

Doc. Want your breakfast now?

MARIE. *(Crosses Left)* Just my fruit juice. I'll drink
it while I dress and have my breakfast later.

Doc. *(Two glasses to table)* Up a little early, aren't
you?

MARIE. I have to get to the library and check out
some books before anyone else gets them.

Doc. Yes, you want to study hard, Marie. Learn to
be a fine artist some day. Paint lots of beautiful pictures. I remember a picture my mother had over the
mantelpiece at home, a picture of a cathedral in a sunset, one of those big cathedrals in Europe somewhere.
Made you feel religious just to look at it.

MARIE. These books aren't for art, they're for biology. I have an exam.

Doc. Biology? Why do they make you take biology?

MARIE. *(Laughs)* It's required. Didn't you have to take biology when you were in college?

Doc. Well—yes, but I was preparing to study medicine, so of course I *had* to take biology and things like that. You see—I was going to be a real doctor then— only I left college my third year.

MARIE. What's the matter? Didn't you like the pre-Med course?

Doc. Yes, of course— I had to give it up.

MARIE. Why?

Doc. *(To stove with roll on plate. Evasive)* I'll put your sweet roll in now, Marie, so it will be nice and warm for you when you want it.

MARIE. Dr. Delaney, you're so nice to your wife, and you're so nice to me; as a matter of fact, you're so nice to everyone. I hope my husband is as nice as you are. Most husbands would never think of getting their own breakfast.

Doc. *(Very pleased with this. Crosses to Left end of table)* —uh—you might as well sit down now and— yes, sit here and I'll serve you your breakfast now, Marie, and we can eat it together, the two of us.

MARIE. *(A light little laugh as she starts dancing away from him)* No, I like to bathe first and feel that I'm all fresh and clean to start the day. I'm going to hop into the tub now. See you later. *(She goes upstairs.)*

Doc. Yes, fresh and clean— (Doc *shows disappointment but goes on in businesslike way setting his breakfast on the table. Door SLAMS upstairs.)*

MARIE. *(Off upstairs)* Mrs. Delaney.

LOLA. *(Off upstairs)* 'Mornin', Honey.

(Then LOLA *comes downstairs. Enter* LOLA. *She is a contrast to* DOC'S *neat cleanliness, and* MARIE'S. *Over a nightdress she wears a lumpy kimona. Her eyes are dim with a morning expression of disillusionment, as though she had had a beautiful*

*dream during the night and found on waking none
of it was true. On her feet are worn, dirty comfies.
To kitchen table, sits in Center chair. Doc Left of
table.)*

LOLA. *(With some self-pity)* I can't sleep late like
I used to. It used to be I could sleep till noon if I
wanted to, but I can't any more. I don't know why.

DOC. Habits change. Here's your fruit juice.

LOLA. *(Taking it)* I oughta be gettin' your breakfast, Doc, instead of you gettin' mine.

DOC. *(Sits Left of table)* I have to get up anyway,
Baby.

LOLA. *(Sadly)* I had another dream last night.

DOC. *(Pours coffee)* About Little Sheba?

LOLA. *(With sudden animation)* It was just as real.
I dreamt I put her on a leash and we walked down
town—to do some shopping. All the people on the street
turned around to admire her, and I felt so proud. Then
we started to walk, and the blocks started going by so
fast that Little Sheba couldn't keep up with me. Suddenly, I looked around and Little Sheba was gone. Isn't
that funny? I looked everywhere for her but I couldn't
find her. And I stood there feeling sort of afraid.
(Pause) Do you suppose that means anything?

DOC. Dreams are funny.

LOLA. Do you suppose it means Little Sheba is going to come back?

DOC. I don't know, Baby.

LOLA. *(Petulant)* I miss her so, Doc. She was such
a cute little puppy. Wasn't she cute?

DOC. *(Smiles with the reminiscence)* Yes, she was
cute.

LOLA. Remember how white and fluffy she used to be
after I gave her a bath? And how her little hind-end
wagged from side to side when she walked?

DOC. *(An appealing memory)* I remember.

LOLA. She was such a cute little puppy. I hated to see
her grow old, didn't you, Doc?

Doc. Yah. Little Sheba should have stayed young forever. Some things should never grow old. That's what it amounts to, I guess.

Lola. She's been gone for such a long time. What do you suppose ever happened to her?

Doc. You can't ever tell.

Lola. *(With anxiety)* Do you suppose she got run over by a car?—Or do you think that old Mrs. Coffman next door poisoned her? I wouldn't be a bit surprised.

Doc. No, Baby. She just disappeared. That's all we know.

Lola. *(Redundantly)* Just vanished one day—vanished into thin air. *(As though in a dream.)*

Doc. I told you I'd find you another one, Baby.

Lola. *(Pessimistically)* You couldn't ever find another puppy as cute as Little Sheba.

Doc. *(Back to reality)* Want an egg?

Lola. No. Just this coffee. *(He pours coffee. Suddenly)* Have you said your prayer, Doc?

Doc. Yes, Baby.

Lola. And did you ask God to be with you—all through the day, and keep you strong?

Doc. Yes, Baby.

Lola. Then God will be with you, Docky. He's been with you almost a year now and I'm so proud of you.

Doc. *(Preening a little)* Sometimes I feel sorta proud of myself.

Lola. Say your prayer, Doc. I like to hear it.

Doc. *(Matter-of-factly)* God grant me the serenity to accept the things I cannot change, courage to change the things I can, and wisdom always to tell the difference.

Lola. That's nice. That's so pretty. When I think of the way you used to drink, always getting into fights, we had so much trouble. I was so scared! I never knew what was going to happen.

Doc. That was a long time ago, Baby.

Lola. I know it, Daddy. I know how you're going to be when you come home now. *(She kisses him lightly.)*

Doc. *I* don't know what I would have done without you.

Lola. And now you've been sober almost a year.

Doc. Yep. A year next month. *(He rises and goes to the sink with coffee cup and two glasses, rinsing them.)*

Lola. Do you have to go to the meeting tonight?

Doc. No. I can skip the meetings now for a while.

Lola. Oh, good! Then you can take me to a movie.

Doc. Sorry, Baby. I'm going out on some Twelfth Step work with Ed Anderson.

Lola. What's that?

Doc. *(Drying the glasses)* I showed you that list of twelve steps the Alcoholics Anonymous have to follow. This is the final one. After you learn to stay dry yourself, then you go out and help other guys that need it.

Lola. Oh!

Doc. *(To sink)* When we help others, we help ourselves.

Lola. I know what you mean. Whenever I help Marie in some way, it makes me feel good.

Doc. Yah. (Lola *gives her cup to* Doc. *Washing it. Turns Right)* Yes but this is a lot different, Baby. When I go out to help some poor drunk, I have to give him courage—to stay sober like I've stayed sober. Most alcoholics are disappointed men— They need courage— *(Turns Left.)*

Lola. You weren't ever disappointed, were you, Daddy?

Doc. *(After a pause)* The important thing is to forget the past and live for the present. And stay sober doing it.

Lola. *(Rises, crosses Left)* Who do you have to help tonight?

Doc. *(To table)* Some guy they picked up on Skid Row last night. *(Gets his coat from back of chair)* They got him at the City Hospital. I kinda dread it.

Lola. I thought you said it helped you.

Doc. *(Puts on coat)* It does, if you can stand it. I did some Twelfth Step work down there once before.

They put alcoholics right in with the crazy people. It's horrible—these men all twisted and shaking—eyes all foggy and full of pain. Some guy there with his fists clamped together, so he couldn't kill anyone. There was a young man, just a *young* man, had scratched his eyes out.

LOLA. *(Cringing)* Don't, Daddy. Seems a shame to take a man there just cause he got drunk.

DOC. Well, they'll sober a man up. That's the important thing. Let's not talk about it any more. *(Crosses to door down Left.)*

LOLA. *(With relief)* Rita Hayworth's on tonight, out at the Plaza. Don't you want to see it?

DOC. Maybe Marie will go with you.

LOLA. Oh, no. She's probably going out with Turk tonight.

DOC. She's too nice a girl to be going out with a guy like Turk.

LOLA. I don't know why, Daddy. Turk's nice. *(Cuts coffee cake.)*

DOC. A guy like that doesn't have any respect for *nice* young girls. You can tell that by looking at him.

LOLA. I never saw Marie object to any of the love-making.

DOC. A big, brawny bozo like Turk, he probably forces her to kiss him.

LOLA. *(Left of table)* Daddy, that's not so at all. I came in the back way once when they were in the living room, and she was kissing him like he was Rudolph Valentino. *(To sink.)*

DOC. *(An angry denial)* Marie is a nice girl.

LOLA. I know she's nice. I just said she and Turk were doing some tall spooning. It wouldn't surprise me any if—

DOC. Honey, I don't want to hear any more about it. *(He crosses up Right.)*

LOLA. You try to make out like every young girl is Jennifer Jones in the Song of Bernadette.

DOC. I do not. I just like to believe that young people

like her are clean and decent— *(Breaks Right to living room.)*

MARIE. *(Comes down stairs)* Hi! *(Gets cup and saucer from drain board. Sits Right of table.)*

LOLA. *(At stove)* There's an extra sweet roll for you this morning, Honey. I didn't want mine.

MARIE. One's plenty, thank you.

DOC. *(To landing)* How soon do you leave this morning?

(LOLA crosses down Right with coffee.)

MARIE. *(Eating)* As soon as I finish my breakfast.

Doc. Well, I'll wait and we can walk to the corner together.

(LOLA crosses up to stove.)

MARIE. Oh, I'm sorry, Doc. Turk's coming by. He has to go to the library, too.

DOC. *(On landing)* Oh, well I'm not going to be competition with a football player. *(Coming to LOLA)* It's a nice spring morning. Wanta walk to the office with me?

LOLA. I look too terrible, Daddy. I ain't even dressed.

Doc. Kiss Daddy goodbye.

LOLA. *(Gets up and kisses him softly)* Bye, bye, Daddy. If you get hungry, come home and I'll have something for you.

MARIE. *(Joking)* Aren't you going to kiss *me*, Dr. Delaney?

(LOLA eggs Doc to go ahead.)

Doc. *(Startled. Hesitates. Forces himself to realize she is only joking and manages to answer)* Can't spend my time kissing *all* the girls.

(MARIE laughs. Doc goes into living room while LOLA

and MARIE *continue talking.* MARIE'S *scarf is tossed over his hat on chair, so he picks it up, then looks at it fondly, holding it in the air, inspecting its delicate gracefulness. He drops it back on chair and starts out by front door.)*

MARIE. I think Dr. Delaney is so nice.

LOLA. *(She is by the closet now, where she keeps a few personal articles. She is getting into a more becoming smock)* When did you say Turk was coming by?

MARIE. Said he'd be here about 9:30. (Doc *exits— hearing the line about* TURK. MARIE *to stove)* That's a pretty smock.

LOLA. *(To table, sits Center chair, changes shoes)* It'll be better to work around the house in.

MARIE. *(To Left of table. Not sounding exactly cheerful)* Mrs. Delaney, I'm expecting a telegram this morning. Would you leave it on my dresser for me when it comes?

LOLA. Sure, Honey. No bad news, I hope.

MARIE. Oh no! It's from Bruce.

LOLA. (MARIE'S *boy friends are one of her liveliest interests)* Oh, your boy friend in Cincinnati. Is he coming to see you?

MARIE. I guess so.

LOLA. I'm just dying to meet him.

MARIE. *(Changing the subject)* Really, Mrs. Delaney, you and Doc have been so nice to me. I just want you to know I appreciate it.

LOLA. Thanks, Honey.

MARIE. You've been like a father and mother to me. I appreciate it.

LOLA. Thanks, Honey. *(To Left.)*

MARIE. Turk was saying just the other night what good sports you both are.

LOLA. *(Brushing hair)* That so?

MARIE. Honest. He said it was just as much fun being with you as with kids our own age.

LOLA. *(Couldn't be more flattered)* Oh, I like that

Turk. He reminds me of a boy I used to know in High
School, Dutch McCoy. Where did you ever meet him?
(Sits Left of table.)

MARIE. *(To above table)* In art class.

LOLA. Turk take art?

MARIE. *(Laughs)* No. It was in a life class. He was
modeling. Lots of the athletes do that. It pays them a
dollar an hour.

LOLA. That's nice.

MARIE. Mrs. Delaney? I've got some corrections to
make in some of my drawings. Is it all right if I bring
Turk home this morning to pose for me? It'll just take
a few minutes.

LOLA. Sure, Honey.

MARIE. *(To sink; replaces cup)* There's a contest on
now. They're giving a prize for the best drawing to
use for advertising the Spring Relays.

LOLA. And. you're going to do a picture of Turk?
That's nice. *(A sudden thought. To stove. A little
secretively)* Doc's gonna be gone tonight. You and
Turk can have the living room if you want to.

MARIE. *(This is a temptation)* O.K. Thanks.
(Crosses Right; exits bedroom.)

> *(LIGHT Q #1: Kitchen down.)*

LOLA. Tell me more about Bruce. *(Follows Right to
bedroom door.)*

MARIE. *(Off in bedroom. Remembering her affinity)*
Well, he comes from one of the best families in Cincinnati. And they have a great big house. And they
have a maid, too. And he's got a wonderful personality.
He makes $300 a month.

LOLA. That so?

MARIE. And he stays at the best hotels. His company
insists on it. *(Enters to Left Center.)*

LOLA. Do you like him as well as Turk? *(Buttons up
back of MARIE's blouse.)*

MARIE. *(Evasive)* Bruce is so dependable, and—he's
a gentleman, too.

LOLA. Are you goin' to marry him, Honey?

MARIE. Maybe, after I graduate from college and he feels he can support a wife and children. I'm going to have lots and lots of children.

LOLA. I wanted children, too. When I lost my baby and found out I couldn't have any more, I didn't know what to do with myself. I wanted to get a job, but Doc wouldn't hear of it.

MARIE. Bruce is going to come into a lot of money some day. His uncle made a fortune in men's garters. *(Exits into her room.)*

LOLA. *(Leans on door frame)* Doc was a rich boy when I married him. His mother left him $25,000 when she died. *(Disillusioned)* It took him a lot to get his office started and everything—then, he got sick. *(She makes a futile gesture; then on the bright side)* But Doc's always good to me—*now.*

MARIE. *(Reenters to Center)* Oh, Doc's a peach.

LOLA. I used to be pretty, something like you. *(She gets her picture from table Left)* I was Beauty Queen of the Senior Class in High School. My dad was awful strict, though. Once he caught me holding hands with that good looking Dutch McCoy. Dad sent Dutch home, and wouldn't let me go out after supper for a whole month. Daddy would never let me go out with boys much. Just because I was pretty. He was afraid all the boys would get the wrong idea—*you* know. I never had any fun at all until I met Doc.

MARIE. Sometimes I'm glad I didn't know my father. Mom always let me do pretty much as I please.

LOLA. Doc was the first boy my dad ever let me go out with. We got married that spring. *(Crosses Left; replaces picture.* MARIE *sits davenport, puts on shoes and socks.)*

MARIE. What did your father think of that?

LOLA. We came right to the city then. And, well, Doc gave up his pre-Med course, and went to Chiropractor School instead.

MARIE. You must have been married awful young.

LOLA. Oh yes. Eighteen.

MARIE. That must have made your father really mad.

LOLA. Yes it did. I never went home after that, but my mother comes down here from Green Valley to visit me sometimes.

TURK. (*Bursts into the front room from outside. He is a young, big, husky, good-looking boy, 19 or 20. He has the openness, the generosity, vigor and health of youth. He's had a little time in the service, but he is not what one would call disciplined. He wears faded dungarees and a T-shirt. He always enters unannounced. He hollers for* MARIE) Hey, Marie! Ready?

MARIE. (*Calling. Runs up Center and exits bedroom, closing door*) Just a minute, Turk.

LOLA. (*Confidentially*) I'll entertain him until you're ready. (*She is by nature coy and kittenish with an attractive man. Picks up papers—stuffs under table Right*) The house is such a mess, Turk! I bet you think I'm an awful housekeeper. Some day I'll surprise you. But you're like one of the family now. (*Pause*) My, you're an early caller.

TURK. Gotta get to the library. Haven't cracked a book for a biology exam and Marie's gotta help me.

LOLA. (*Unconsciously admiring his stature and physique and looking him over*) My. I'd think you'd be chilly running around in just that thin little shirt.

TURK. Me? I go like this in the middle of winter.

LOLA. Well, you're a big husky man.

TURK. (*Laughs*) Oh, I'm a brute, *I* am.

LOLA. (*Sits chair Right*) You should be out in Hollywood making those Tarzan movies.

TURK. I had enough of that place when I was in the Navy.

LOLA. (*With no idea what he's talking about*) That so?

TURK. (*Calling*) Hey, Marie, hurry up.

MARIE. (*Off*) Oh, be patient, Turk.

TURK. (*To* LOLA) She doesn't realize how busy I am. I'll only have a half hour to study at most. I gotta report to the coach at 10:30.

LOLA. What are you in training for now?

TURK. Spring track. They got me throwing the javelin.

LOLA. The javelin? What's that?

TURK. *(Laughs at her ignorance)* It's a big, long lance. *(Assumes the magnificent position)* You hold it like this, erect—then you let go and it goes singing through the air, and lands yards away, if you're any good at it, and sticks in the ground, quivering like an arrow. I won the State Championship last year.

LOLA. *(She has watched as though fascinated)* My!

TURK. *(Very generous)* Get Marie to take you to the track field some afternoon, and you can watch me.

LOLA. That would be thrilling.

MARIE. *(Comes dancing in)* Hi, Turk.

TURK. Hi, juicey.

LOLA. *(As the YOUNG COUPLE moves to the doorway)* Remember, Marie, you and Turk can have the room tonight. All to yourselves. You can play the radio and dance and make a plate of fudge, or anything you want.

MARIE. *(To TURK)* O.K.?

TURK. *(With eagerness)* Sure.

MARIE. Let's go. *(Exits.)*

LOLA. 'Bve, kids.

TURK. 'Bye, Mrs. Delaney. *(Gives her a chuck under the chin)* You're a swell skirt.

(LOLA *couldn't be more flattered. For a moment she is breathless. They speed out the door and LOLA stands, sadly watching them depart. Then a sad, vacant look comes over her face. Her arms drop in a gesture of futility. Slowly she walks out on the front porch and calls.)*

LOLA. Little Sheba! Come, Little She-ba. Come back —come back, Little Sheba! *(She waits for a few moments, then comes wearily back into the house, closing the door behind her. SOUND Q #1: Airplane 1 3/4.*

Now the morning has caught up with her. She goes to the kitchen, kicks off her pumps and gets back into comfies. The sight of the dishes on the drainboard depresses her. Clearly she is bored to death. Then the TELEPHONE rings with the promise of relieving her. She answers it) Hello— Oh no, you've got the wrong number— Oh, that's all right. *(Again it looks hopeless. She hears the* POSTMAN. *Now her spirits are lifted. She runs to the front door, opens it and awaits him. When he's within distance, she lets loose a barrage of welcome)* 'Morning, Mr. Postman.

POSTMAN. *(Entering to porch)* 'Morning, Ma'am.

LOLA. You better have something for me today. Sometimes I think you don't even know I live here. You haven't left me anything for two whole weeks. If you can't do better than that, I'll just have to get a new postman.

POSTMAN. *(On the porch)* You'll have to get someone to write you some letters, lady. Nope, nothing for you.

LOLA. Well, I was only joking. You knew I was joking, didn't you. I bet you're thirsty. You come right in here and I'll bring you a glass of cold water. *(Enters living room)* Come in and sit down for a few minutes and rest your feet a while.

POSTMAN. I'll take you up on that, Lady. *(Coming in)* I've worked up quite a thirst.

LOLA. You sit down. I'll be back in just a minute. *(Goes to kitchen, gets pitcher out of refrigerator and brings it back.)*

POSTMAN. Spring is turnin' into summer awful soon.

LOLA. You feel free to stop here and ask me for a drink of water any time you want to. (POSTMAN *sits down Right. Pouring drink)* That's what we're all here for, isn't it? To make each other comfortable?

POSTMAN. Thank you, Ma'am.

LOLA. *(Clinging, not wanting to be left alone so soon; she hurries her conversation to hold him)* You haven't been our postman very long, have you?

POSTMAN. *(She hands him a glass of water, stands holding pitcher as he drinks)* No.

LOLA. You postmen have things pretty nice, don't you? I hear you get nice pensions after you been working for the government twenty years. I think that's dandy. It's a *good* job, too. *(Pours him a second glass)* You may get tired but I think it's good for a man to be outside and get a lot of exercise. Keeps him strong and healthy. My husband, he's a doctor, a *chiro*practor; he has to stay inside his office all day long. The only exercise he gets is rubbin' people's backbones. *(They laugh. LOLA crosses Left to table, leaves pitcher)* It makes his hands strong. He's got the strongest hands you ever did see. But he's got a poor digestion. I keep tellin' him he oughta get some fresh air once in a while and some exercise. (POSTMAN *rises as if to go, and this hurries her into a more absorbing monologue)* You know what? My husband is an Alcoholics Anonymous. He doesn't care if I tell you that 'cause he's proud of it. He hasn't touched a drop in almost a year. All that time we've had a quart of whiskey in the pantry for company and he hasn't even gone near it. Doesn't even want to. You know, alcoholics can't drink like ordinary people; they're *allergic* to it. It affects them different. They get started drinking and can't stop. Liquor transforms them. Sometimes they get mean and violent and wanta fight—but if they let liquor alone, they're perfectly all right, just like you and me. (POSTMAN *tries to leave.)* You should have seen Doc before he gave it up. He lost all his patients, wouldn't even go to the office; just wanted to stay drunk all day long and he'd come home at night and— You just wouldn't believe it if you saw him now. He's got his patients all back, and he's just doing fine.

POSTMAN. Sure I know Dr. Delaney. I deliver his office mail. He's a fine man.

LOLA. Oh thanks. You don't ever drink, do you?

POSTMAN. Oh, a few beers once in a while. *(He is ready to go.)*

LOLA. Well, I guess that stuff doesn't do any of us any good.

POSTMAN. No. *(Crosses down for mailbag on floor Center)* Well, good day, Ma'am.

LOLA. Say, you got any kids?

POSTMAN. Three grandchildren.

LOLA. *(Getting it from table Left)* We don't have any kids, and we got this toy in a box of breakfast food. Why don't you take it home to them?

POSTMAN. Why, that's very kind of you, Ma'am. *(He takes it, and goes.)*

LOLA. Goodbye, Mr. Postman.

POSTMAN. *(On porch)* I'll see that you get a letter, if I have to write it myself.

(LIGHT Q #2: Kitchen up.)

LOLA. Thanks. Goodbye. *(Left alone, she crosses down, turns on radio. Then she goes to kitchen to start dishes, showing her boredom in the half-hearted way she washes them. Takes water back to ice box. Then she spies MRS. COFFMAN hanging baby clothes on lines just outside kitchen door. Goes to door)* My, you're a busy woman this morning, Mrs. Coffman.

MRS. COFFMAN. *(German accent. She is outside, but sticks her head in for some of the following)* Being busy is being happy.

LOLA. I guess so.

MRS. COFFMAN. I don't have it as easy as you. When you got seven kids to look after, you got no time to sit around the house, Mrs. Delaney.

LOLA. I s'pose not.

MRS. COFFMAN. But you don't hear me complain.

LOLA. Oh, no. You never complain. *(Pause. To porch door)* I guess my little doggie's gone for good, Mrs. Coffman. I sure miss her.

MRS. COFFMAN. The only way to keep from missing one dog is to get another.

LOLA. *(To sink, turns off water)* Oh, I never could find another doggy as cute as Little Sheba.

MRS. COFFMAN. *(In)* Did you put an ad in the paper?

LOLA. For two whole weeks. No one answered it. It's just like she vanished—into thin air. *(She likes this metaphor)* Every day, though, I go out on the porch and call her. You can't tell; she might be around. Don't you think?

MRS. COFFMAN. You should get busy and forget her. You should get busy, Mrs. Delaney.

LOLA. Yes, I'm going to. I'm going to start my spring house-cleaning one of these days real soon. Why don't you come in and have a cup of coffee with me, Mrs. Coffman, and we can chat a while.

MRS. COFFMAN. I got work to do, Mrs. Delaney. I got work. *(Exits.)*

(LOLA *turns from the window, annoyed at her rejection. Is about to start in on the dishes when the* MILKMAN *arrives. She opens the back door and detains him.)*

MILKMAN. 'Morning, Mrs. Coffman.

MRS. COFFMAN. 'Morning.

LOLA. Hello there, Mr. Milkman. How are you to-day?

MILKMAN. 'Morning, Lady.

LOLA. I think I'm going to want a few specials today. Can you come in a minute? *(To icebox.)*

MILKMAN. *(He probably is used to her. He is not a handsome man but husky and attractive in his uniform. Coming in. Follows by sink)* What'll it be?

LOLA. *(Icebox)* Well, now, let's see. Have you got any cottage cheese?

MILKMAN. We always got cottage cheese, Lady. *(Crosses up, showing her card)* All you gotta do is check the items on the card and we leave 'em. Now I gotta go back to the truck. *(To Center.)*

LOLA. Now, don't scold me. I always mean to do that but you're always here before I think of it. Now, I guess I'll need some coffee cream, too—half a pint.

MILKMAN. Coffee cream. O.K.

LOLA. Now let me see— Oh, yes, I want a quart of buttermilk. My husband has liked buttermilk ever since he stopped drinking. My husband's an alcoholic. Had to give it up. Did I ever tell you?

MILKMAN. Yes, Lady. (*Starts to go. She follows.*)

LOLA. Now he can't get enough to eat. Eats six times a day. He comes home in the middle of the morning, and I fix him a snack. In the middle of the afternoon he has a malted milk with an egg in it. And then another snack before he goes to bed.

MILKMAN. What'd ya know?

LOLA. Keeps his energy up.

MILKMAN. I'll bet. Anything else, Lady?

LOLA. No, I guess not.

MILKMAN. (*Going out*) Be back in a jiffy. (*Gives her slip. Exits.*)

LOLA. I'm just so sorry I put you to so much extra work. (*He returns shortly with dairy products.*) After this I'm going to do my best to remember to check the card. I don't think it's right to put people to extra work. (*To icebox, puts things away.*)

MILKMAN. (*Smiles, is willing to forget*) That's all right, Lady. (*To chair Right of table; foot on same.*)

LOLA. Maybe you'd like a piece of cake or a sandwich. Got some awfully good cold cuts in the icebox.

MILKMAN. No, thanks, Lady.

LOLA. Or maybe you'd like a cup of coffee.

MILKMAN. No, thanks. (*He's checking the items, putting them on the bill.*)

LOLA. You're just a young man. You oughta be going to college. I think everyone should have an education. Do you like your job?

MILKMAN. It's O.K. (*Changes to Left foot, looks at LOLA.*)

LOLA. You're a husky young man. You oughta be out in Hollywood making those Tarzan movies.

MILKMAN. (*Steps back, Center. Feels a little flattered*) When I first began on this job I didn't get enough exercise, so I started working out on the bar bell.

LOLA. Bar bells?

MILKMAN. Keeps you in trim.

LOLA. *(Fascinated)* Yes, I imagine.

MILKMAN. I sent my picture in to Strength and Health last month. *(Proudly)* It's a physique study! If they print it, I'll bring you a copy.

LOLA. Oh, will you? I think we should all take better care of ourselves, don't you?

MILKMAN. If you ask me, Lady, that's what's wrong with the world today. We're not taking care of ourselves.

LOLA. I wouldn't be surprised.

MILKMAN. Every morning I do forty push-ups before I eat my breakfast.

LOLA. Push-ups?

MILKMAN. Like this. *(He spreads himself on the floor and demonstrates, doing three rapid push-ups. LOLA couldn't be more fascinated. Then he springs to his feet)* That's good for shoulder development. Wanta feel my shoulders?

LOLA. Why—why, yes. *(He makes one arm tense and puts her hand on his shoulder.)* Why, it's just like a rock.

MILKMAN. I can do seventy-nine without stopping.

LOLA. Seventy-nine!

MILKMAN. Now feel my arm.

LOLA. *(Does so)* Goodness!

MILKMAN. You wouldn't believe what a puny kid I was. Sickly, no appetite.

LOLA. Is that a fact! And, my! Look at you now.

MILKMAN. *(Very proud)* Shucks, any man could do the same—if he just takes care of himself.

(HORN—2 beeps.)

LOLA. Oh sure, sure.

MILKMAN. There's my buddy. I gotta beat it. *(Picks*

up his things, shakes hands, leaves hurriedly) See you
tomorrow, Lady.

LOLA. 'Bye. *(She watches him from kitchen window
until he gets out of sight. There is a look of some wonder on her face, an emptiness, as though she were un-
able to understand anything that ever happened to her.
She looks at clock, runs into living room, turns on radio.
A pulsating tom-tom is heard as a theme introduction.
Then the* ANNOUNCER.)

> (LOLA *crosses* R. *Kitchen door light Q #3.
> Start record Q #2. Ice box door close.* LOLA
> *at radio. Sound Q #2 6½-9-3-9.)*

ANNOUNCER. *(In dramatic voice)* TA-BOOoooo!
(Now in a very soft, highly personalized voice. LOLA
sits davenport, eats candy.) It's Ta-boo, radio listeners,
your fifteen minutes of temptation. *(An alluring voice)*
Won't you join me? (LOLA *swings feet up.)* Won't you
leave behind your routine, the dull cares that make up
your day-to-day existence, the little worries, the un-
certainties, the confusions of the work-a-day world and
follow me where pagan spirits hold sway, where lithe
natives dance on a moon-enchanted isle, where palm
trees sway with the restless ocean tide, restless surging
on the white shore. Won't you come along? *(More tom-
tom. Now in an oily voice)* But remember, it's TA-
BOOOOOooooo-OOO! *(Now the tom-tom again, going into a sensual, primitive rhythm melody.)*

*(LOLA has been transfixed from the beginning of the
program. She lies down on the davenport, listening.
Then, slowly, growing more and more comfortable.)*

WESTERN UNION BOY. *(At door)* Telegram for Miss
Maria Buckholder.   *(SOUND to 3.)*
LOLA. She's not here.
WESTERN UNION BOY. Sign here.   *(SOUND to 9.)*

(LOLA does, then she closes the door and brings the en-

velope into the house, looking at it wonderingly. This is a major temptation for her. She puts the envelope on the table down Right, but can't resist looking at it. Finally she gives in and takes it to the kitchen to steam it open. Then MARIE *and* TURK *burst into the room.* LOLA, *confused, wonders what to do with the telegram, then decides, just in the nick of time, to jam it in her apron pocket.)*

MARIE. Mrs. Delaney! *(Turns off radio. At the sound of* MARIE'S *voice,* LOLA, *embarrassedly, runs in to greet them)* —mind if we turn your parlor into an art studio?

LOLA. Sure, go right ahead. Hi, Turk.

(TURK *gives a wave of his arm.)*

MARIE. *(To* TURK, *indicating her bedroom)* You can change in there, Turk.

(TURK *goes into bedroom.)*

LOLA. *(To Right Center. Puzzled)* Change?

MARIE. He's gotta take off his clothes.

LOLA. Huh? *(To Right, closes door.)*

MARIE. These drawings are for my life class.

LOLA. *(Consoled but still mystified. To Left by table)* Oh.

MARIE. *(Sits davenport)* Turk's the best male model we've had all year. Lotsa athletes pose for us 'cause they've all got muscles. They're easier to draw.

LOLA. You mean—he's gonna pose *naked?*

MARIE. *(Laughs)* No. The women do, but the men are always more proper. Turk's going to pose in his track suit.

LOLA. *(Breaks to Left end of davenport)* Oh. *(Almost to herself)* The women pose nude but the men don't. *(This strikes her as a startling inconsistency)* If it's all right for a woman, it oughta be for a man.

MARIE. *(Businesslike)* The man always keeps covered. *(Calling to* TURK*)* Hurry up, Turk.

TURK. *(With all his muscles in place, he comes out. He is not at all self-conscious about his semi-nudity. His body is something he takes very much for granted. To down Right Center.* LOLA *is a little dazed by the spectacle of flesh.)* How do you want this lovely body? Same pose I took in Art Class?

MARIE. Yah. Over there where I can get more light on you.

TURK. *(Opens door. Starts pose)* Anything in the house I can use for a javelin?

MARIE. Is there, Mrs. Delaney?

LOLA. How about the broom?

TURK. O.K.

(LOLA *runs out to get it.* TURK *goes to her in kitchen, takes it, returns to living room and resumes pose.)*

MARIE. *(From davenport, studying* TURK *in relation to her sketch-pad. To Right—moves his leg)* Your left foot a little more this way. *(Studying it)* O.K., hold it. *(Starts sketching rapidly and industriously.)*

LOLA. *(Looks on, lingeringly. Starts unwillingly into kitchen, changes her mind and returns to the scene of action.* MARIE *and* TURK *are too busy to comment.* LOLA *looks at sketch, inspecting it)* Well—that's real pretty, Marie. (MARIE *is silent.* LOLA *moves closer to look at the drawing)* It—it's real artistic. *(Pause)* I wish *I* was artistic.

TURK. Baby, I can't hold this pose very long at a time.

MARIE. Rest whenever you feel like it.

TURK. O.K.!

MARIE. *(To* LOLA*)* If I make a good drawing, they'll use it for the posters for the Spring Relays.

LOLA. Ya. You told me.

MARIE. *(To* TURK*)* After I'm finished with these sketches I won't have to bother you any more.

TURK. No bother. *(Rubs his shoulder—he poses)* Hard pose, though. Gets me in the shoulder.

(MARIE pays no attention. LOLA crosses up Right, peers at him so closely he becomes a little self-conscious and breaks pose. This also breaks LOLA's concentration.)

LOLA. I'll heat you up some coffee. *(Goes to kitchen.)*

TURK. *(Crosses down Left to MARIE. Softly to MARIE)* Hey, can't you keep her out of here? She makes me feel naked.

MARIE. *(Laughs)* I can't keep her out of her own house, can I?

TURK. Didn't she ever see a man before?

MARIE. Not a big, beautiful man like you, Turky. *(TURK smiles, is flattered by any recognition of his physical worth, takes it as an immediate invitation to lovemaking. Pulling her up, he kisses her as DOC comes up on porch. MARIE pushes TURK away)* Turk, get back in your corner.   *(LIGHT Q #4. Kitchen up.)*

DOC. *(Comes in from outside. Cheerily)* Hi, everyone.

MARIE. Hi.

TURK. Hi, Doc. (DOC *then sees* TURK, *feels immediate resentment. Goes into kitchen to* LOLA) What's goin' on here?

LOLA. *(Getting cups)* Oh, hello, Daddy. Marie's doin' a drawin'.

DOC. *(Trying to size the situation up.* MARIE *and* TURK *are too busy to speak.)* Oh.

LOLA. I've just heated up the coffee. Want some?

DOC. Yeah. *(To table)* What happened to Turk's clothes?

LOLA. Marie's doing some drawings for her *life* classes, Doc.

DOC. *(Sits table Center)* Can't she draw him with his clothes on?

LOLA. *(Crossing with coffee. Very professional now)*

No, Doc, it's not the same. See, it's a *life* class. They draw bodies. They all do it, right in the classroom.

Doc. Why, Marie's just a young girl; she shouldn't be drawing things like that. I don't care if they do teach it at college. It's not right.

Lola. *(Disclaiming responsibility)* I don't know, Doc.

Turk. *(Turns and faces upstage)* I'm tired.

Marie. *(Moving and squats at his feet)* Just let me finish the foot.

Doc. Why doesn't she draw something else—a bowl of flowers or a cathedral—or a sunset.

Lola. All she told me, Doc, was if she made a good drawing of Turk, they'd use it for the posters for the Spring Relay. *(Pause)* So I guess they don't want sunsets.

Doc. What if someone walked into the house now? What would they think?

Lola. Daddy, Marie just asked me if it was all right if Turk came and posed for her. Now that's all she said, and I said O.K. But if you think it's wrong, I won't let them do it again.

Doc. I just don't like it.

Marie. Hold it a minute more.

Turk. O.K.

Lola. Well, then you speak to Marie about it if—

Doc. *(He'd never mention anything disapprovingly to* Marie*)* No, Baby. I couldn't do that.

Lola. *(Sits Left of table)* Well then—

Doc. Besides, it's not her fault. If those college people make her do drawings like that, I suppose she has to do them. I just don't think it's right she should have to, that's all.

Lola. Well, if you think it's wrong—

Doc. *(Ready to dismiss it)* Never mind.

Lola. I don't see any harm in it, Daddy.

Doc. Forget it.

Lola. *(To ice box)* Would you like some buttermilk?

Doc. Thanks.

MARIE. *(Finishes sketch)* O.K. That's all I can do for today.

TURK. Is there anything I can do for you?

MARIE. Yes—get your clothes on.

TURK. O.K., Coach. (TURK *exits to bedroom.* MARIE *sits down Right.)*

LOLA. *(Standing Left of* DOC) You know what Marie said, Doc? She said that the women posed naked, but the men don't.

DOC. Why, of course, Honey.

LOLA. Why is that?

DOC. *(Stumped)* —well—

LOLA. If it's all right for a woman, it oughta be for a man. But the man always keeps covered. That's what she said.

DOC. Well, that's the way it should be, Honey. A man, after all, is a man, and he—well, he has to protect himself.   *(WARN Curtain.)*

LOLA. And a woman doesn't?

DOC. It's different, Honey.

LOLA. Is it? I've got a secret, Doc. Bruce is comin'.

DOC. Is that so?

LOLA. *(After a glum silence)* You know—Marie's boy friend from Cincinnati. I promised Marie a long time ago, when her fiance came to town, dinner was on me. So I'm getting out the best china and cook the best meal you ever sat down to.

DOC. When did she get the news?

LOLA. The telegram came this morning.

DOC. That's fine. That Bruce sounds to me like just the fellow for her. I think I'll go in and congratulate her.

LOLA. *(Nervous)* Not now, Doc.

DOC. Why not?

LOLA. Well, Turk's there. It might make him feel embarrassed.

DOC. Well, why doesn't Turk clear out now that Bruce is coming? What's he hanging around for? She's engaged to marry Bruce, isn't she?

(TURK *enters from bedroom and goes to* MARIE, *starting to make advances.*)

LOLA. Marie's just doing a picture of him, Doc.
DOC. You always stick up for him. You encourage him.
LOLA. Shhh, Daddy. Don't get upset.
DOC. *(Very angrily)* All right, but if anything happens to the girl I'll never forgive you.

(DOC *goes upstairs.* TURK *then grabs* MARIE, *kisses her passionately.*)

(*SOUND Q #3.*)

FAST CURTAIN

ACT ONE

SCENE II

(SOUND out. FOOTS out. Kitchen chandelier on. Kitchen areas up. Living room lamps on. Living areas low.)

The same evening, after supper. Outside it is dark. There has been an almost miraculous transformation of the entire house. LOLA, *apparently, has been working hard and fast all day. The rooms are spotlessly clean and there are such additions as new lampshades, fresh curtains, etc. In the kitchen all the enamel surfaces glisten, and piles of junk that have lain around for months have been disposed of.* LOLA *and* DOC *are in the kitchen, he washing up the dishes and she puttering around putting the finishing touches on her housecleaning.*

LOLA. *(At stove)* There's still some beans left. Do you want them, Doc?

Doc. *(At sink)* I had enough.

Lola. I hope you got enough to eat tonight, Daddy. I been so busy cleaning I didn't have time to fix you much.

Doc. I wasn't very hungry.

Lola. *(To table, cleaning up)* You know what? Mrs. Coffman said I could come over and pick all the lilacs I wanted for my centerpiece tomorrow. Isn't that nice? I don't think she poisoned Little Sheba, do you?

Doc. I never did think so, Baby. Where'd you get the new curtains?

Lola. I went out and bought them this afternoon. Aren't they pretty? Be careful of the woodwork; it's been varnished.

Doc. How come, Honey?

Lola. *(Gets broom and dust pan from closet)* Bruce is comin'. I figured I had to do my spring house-cleaning sometime.

Doc. You got all this done in one day? The house hasn't looked like this in years.

Lola. I can be a good housekeeper when I want to be, can't I, Doc?

Doc. *(Kneels, holding dustpan for* Lola*)* I never had any complaints. Where's Marie now?

Lola. I don't know, Doc. I haven't seen her since she left here this morning with Turk.

Doc. *(Rises. A look of disapproval)* Marie's too good to be wasting her time with him.

Lola. Daddy, Marie can take care of herself. Don't worry. *(To closet—returns broom.)*

Doc. *(Goes into living room)* 'Bout time for Fibber McGee and Molly.

Lola. *(Untying apron. To closet and then to back door)* Daddy, I'm gonna run over to Mrs. Coffman's and see if she's got any silver polish. I'll be right back. *(Start record Q 4. Sound Q #4. AVA 6-7-9-6.)*

(Doc goes to radio. Lola *exits. At the radio* Doc *starts twisting the dial. He rejects one noisy program*

*after another, then very unexpectedly he comes
across a rendition of Shubert's famous "Ave
Maria," sung in a high soprano voice. Probably he
has encountered the piece before somewhere, but
it is now making its first impression on him. Sits
davenport. Gradually he is transported into a
world of ethereal beauty which he never knew
existed. He listens intently. The music has ex-
pressed some ideal of beauty he never fully realized
and he is even a little mystified. Then LOLA comes
in the back door, letting it slam, breaking the spell;
and announcing in a loud, energetic voice:)*

LOLA. *(Comes into living room)* Isn't it funny? I'm
not a bit tired tonight. You'd think after working so
hard all day I'd be pooped.

    *(LOLA at switch. Light Q #1. Living room
    chandelier on. Areas up.)*

DOC. *(He cringes)* Baby, don't use that word.

LOLA. *(Sets silver polish down and joins DOC on
davenport)* I'm sorry, Doc. I hear Marie and Turk say
it all the time, and I thought it was kinda cute.

DOC. It—it sounds vulgar.

LOLA. *(Kisses DOC)* I won't say it again, Daddy.
Where's Fibber McGee?   *(Start record Q 5.)*

DOC. Not quite time yet.

LOLA. *(Sits chair down Right)* Let's get some peppy
music.

DOC. *(Tuning in a sentimental dance band)* That
what you want?

    (SOUND Q #5—10-2½. Master 50 low.)

LOLA. That's O.K. (Doc takes a pack of cards off
*radio, returns to davenport and starts shuffling them
very deftly.)* I love to watch you shuffle cards, Daddy.
You use your hands so gracefully. *(She watches closely. Rises, crosses to DOC)* Do me one of your card
tricks.

DOC. Baby, you've seen them all.

LOLA. But I never get tired of them.

Doc. O.K. Take a card. (LOLA *does.*) Keep it now. Don't tell me what it is.

LOLA. I won't.

Doc. (*Shuffling cards again*) Now put it back in the deck. I won't look. (*He closes his eyes.*)

LOLA. (*With childish delight*) All right.

Doc. Put it back.

LOLA. Uh-huh.

Doc. O.K. (*Shuffles cards again, cutting them, taking top half off, exposing* LOLA's *card, to her astonishment*) That your card?

LOLA. (*Unbelievingly*) Daddy, how did you do it?

Doc. Baby, I've pulled that trick on you dozens of times.

LOLA. But I never understand how you do it.

Doc. Very simple.

LOLA. Docky, show me how you do that.

Doc. (*You can forgive him a harmless feeling of superiority*) Try it for yourself. (*Rises; crosses Right.*)

LOLA. Doc, you're clever. I never could do it.

Doc. Nothing to it.

LOLA. There is *too*. Show me how you do it, Doc.

Doc. And give away all my secrets? (*Sits down Right*) It's a gift, Honey. A magic gift.

LOLA. Can't you give it to me?   (*SOUND off.*)

Doc. (*Picks up newspaper*) A man has to keep some things to himself.

LOLA. It's not a gift at all, it's just some trick you *learned*.

Doc. O.K., Baby, any way you want to look at it.
                              (*Start record Q #6.*)

LOLA. Let's have some music. How soon do you have to meet Ed Anderson?   (*SOUND Q #6. 3-2-2½-2.*)

Doc. (*Turns on radio*) I still got a little time. (*Pleased.*)

LOLA. Marie's going to be awfully happy when she sees the house all fixed up. She can entertain Bruce here when he comes, and maybe we could have a little party here and you can do your card tricks.

Doc. O.K.

Lola. I think a young girl should be able to bring her friends home.

Doc. Sure.

Lola. We never liked to sit around the house 'cause the folks always stayed there with us. *(Rises—starts dancing alone)* Remember the dances we used to go to, Daddy?

Doc. Sure.

Lola. We had awful good times—for a while, didn't we?

Doc. Yes, Baby.

Lola. Remember the homecoming dance, when Charlie Kettlekamp and I won the Charleston Contest?

Doc. Yah. Please, Honey, I'm trying to read.

Lola. And you got mad at him cause he thought he should take me home afterwards.

Doc. I did not.

Lola. Yes, you did. Charlie was all right, Doc, really he was. You were just jealous.

Doc. I *wasn't* jealous.

Lola. *(She has become very coy and flirtatious now, an old dog playing old tricks)* You got jealous. Every time we went out any place and I even looked at another boy. There was never anything between Charlie and me; there never was.

Doc. That was a long time ago—

Lola. Lots of other boys called me up for dates—Sammy Knight—Hand Biederman—Dutch McCoy.

Doc. Sure, Baby. You were the "it" girl.

Lola. *(Pleading for his attention now)* But I saved all my dates for *you*, didn't I, Doc?

Doc. *(Trying to joke)* As far as *I* know, Baby.

Lola. *(Hurt)* Daddy, I did. You *got* to believe that. I never took a date with any other boy but you.

Doc. *(A little weary and impatient)* That's all forgotten now. *(Turns off radio.)* *(SOUND switch off.)*

LOLA. How can you talk that way, Doc? That was the happiest time of our lives.

DOC. *(Disapprovingly)* Honey!

LOLA. *(At the window)* That was a nice spring. The trees were so heavy and green and the air smelled so sweet. Remember the walks we used to take, down to the old chapel, where it was so quiet and still? *(Sits davenport.)*

DOC. In the spring a young man's fancy turns— pretty fancy.

LOLA. *(In the same tone of reverie)* I was pretty then, wasn't I, Doc? Remember the first time you kissed me? You were scared as a young girl, I believe, Doc; you trembled so. *(She is being very soft and delicate. Caught in the reverie, he chokes a little and cannot answer.)* We'd been going together all year and you were always so shy. Then for the first time you grabbed me and kissed me. Tears came to your eyes, Doc, and you said you'd love me forever and ever. Remember? You said—if I didn't marry you, you wanted to die— I remember 'cause it scared me for anyone to say a thing like that.

DOC. *(In a repressed tone)* Yes, Baby.

LOLA. And when the evening came on, we stretched out on the cool grass and you kissed me all night long.

DOC. *(Rises. Opens door)* Baby, you've got to forget those things. That was twenty years ago.

LOLA. I'll soon be forty. Those years have just vanished—vanished into thin air.

DOC. Yes.

LOLA. Just disappeared—like Little Sheba. *(Pause)* Maybe you're sorry you married me now. You didn't know I was going to get old and fat and sloppy—

DOC. Oh, Baby!

LOLA. It's the truth. That's what I am. But I didn't know it, either. Are you sorry you married me, Doc?

DOC. Of course not.

LOLA. *(Rises; crosses to* DOC) <u>I mean, are you sorry you *had* to marry me?</u>

DOC. *(Onto porch)* We were never going to talk about that, Baby.

LOLA. *(Following* DOC *out)* You *were* the first one, Daddy, the *only* one. I'd just die if you didn't believe that.

DOC. *(Tenderly)* I know, Baby.

LOLA. You were so nice and so proper, Doc; I thought nothing we could do together could ever be wrong—or make us unhappy. Do you think we did wrong, Doc?

DOC. *(Consoling)* No, Baby, of course I don't.

LOLA. I don't think anyone knows about it except my folks, do you?

DOC. *(Crossing in to up Right)* Of course not, Baby.

LOLA. *(Follows in)* I wish the baby had lived, Doc. I don't think that woman knew her business, do you, Doc?

DOC. I guess not.

LOLA. If we'd gone to a doctor, she would have lived, don't you think?

DOC. Perhaps.

LOLA. A doctor wouldn't have known we'd just got married, would he? Why were we so afraid?

DOC. *(Sits davenport)* We were just kids. Kids don't know how to look after things.

LOLA. *(Sits davenport)* If we'd had the baby she'd be a young girl now; then maybe you'd have *saved* your money, Doc, and she could be going to college— like Marie.

DOC. Baby, what's done is done.

LOLA. It must make you feel bad at times to think you had to give up being a doctor and to think you don't have any money like you used to.

DOC. *(Takes stage)* No—no, Baby. We should never feel bad about what's past. What's in the past can't be helped. You—you've got to forget it and live for the present. If you can't forget the past, you stay in it and never get out. I might be a big M.D. today, instead of a chiropractor; we might have had a family to raise and be with us now; I might still have a lot of money if I'd used my head and invested it carefully, instead of gettin' drunk every night. We might have a nice house, and comforts, and friends. But we don't have any of those things. So what! We gotta keep on living, don't we? I can't stop just 'cause I made a few mistakes. I gotta keep goin'—somehow.

LOLA. Sure, Daddy.

DOC. *(Sighs and wipes brow)* I—I wish you wouldn't ask me questions like that, Baby. Let's not talk about it any more. I gotta keep goin', and not let things upset me, or—or—*I* saw enough at the City Hospital to keep me sober for a long time.

LOLA. I'm sorry, Doc. I didn't mean to upset you.

DOC. I'm not upset.

LOLA. What time'll you be home tonight?

DOC. 'Bout eleven o'clock.

LOLA. I wish you didn't have to go tonight. I feel kinda lonesome.

DOC. *(Sits davenport)* Ya, so do I, Baby, but sometime soon we'll go *out* together. I kinda hate to go to those night clubs and places since I stopped drinking, but some night I'll take you out to dinner.

LOLA. Oh, will you, Daddy?

DOC. We'll get dressed up and go to the Windermere and have a fine dinner, and dance between courses.

LOLA. *(Eagerly)* Let's do, Daddy. I got a little money saved up. I got about forty dollars out in the kitchen. We can take that if you need it.

DOC. I'll have plenty of money the first of the month.

LOLA. (LOLA *has made a quick response to the change of mood, seeing a future evening of carefree fun)* What are we sitting round here so serious for? *(To radio)* Let's have some music. *(SOUND Q #7—9-7-10-7-5-3-2-1 ¾. LOLA gets a lively foxtrot on the radio, dances with* DOC. *They begin dancing vigorously, as though to dispense with the sadness of the preceding dialogue, but slowly it winds them and leaves* LOLA *panting)* We oughta go dancing—all the time, Docky—It'd be good for us. Maybe if I danced more often I'd lose—some of—this fat. I remember—I used to be able to dance like this—all night—and not even notice—it. (LOLA *breaks into a Charleston routine as of yore)* Remember the Charleston, Daddy?

(DOC *is clapping his hands in rhythm. Then* MARIE *bursts in through the front door, the personification of the youth that* LOLA *is trying to recapture.)*
                                    (SOUND #7.)
Doc. Hi, Marie!
MARIE. *(Right Center)* What are you trying to do, a jig, Mrs. Delaney?

(MARIE *doesn't intend her remark to be cruel, but it wounds* LOLA. LOLA *stops abruptly in her dancing, losing all the fun she has been able to create for herself. She feels she might cry, so to hide her feelings she hurries quietly out to kitchen.* DOC *and* MARIE *do not notice.)*

MARIE. *(Noticing the change in atmosphere)* Hey, what's been happening around here?
Doc. Lola got to feeling industrious. You oughta see the kitchen.   *(SOUND to #5.)*
MARIE. *(Running to kitchen, where she is too observant of the changes to notice* LOLA *is weeping in corner.* LOLA, *of course, straightens up as soon as* MARIE *enters.)* What got into you, Mrs. Delaney? You've done wonders with the house. It looks marvellous.
LOLA. *(Quietly)* Thanks, Marie.
MARIE. *(Darting back into living room)* I can hardly believe I'm in the same place.
Doc. *(Right. Meaning* BRUCE) Think your boy friend'll like it?   *(SOUND to #3.)*

MARIE. *(Thinking of* TURK) You know how men are. Turk never notices things like that. *(Starts into her own room, blowing a kiss to* DOC *on her way.)*

*(*LOLA *comes back in, dabbing at her eyes.)*

DOC. Turk? (MARIE *is gone; turning to* LOLA) What's the matter, Honey? *(To* LOLA, *at stairs.)*
LOLA. I don't know.
DOC. Feel bad about something?
LOLA. I·didn't want her to see me dancing that way. Makes me feel sorta silly.
DOC. Why, you're a fine dancer.
LOLA. I feel kinda silly.
MARIE. *(Jumps back into the room with her telegram)* My telegram's here. When did it come?
LOLA. It came about an hour ago, Honey.

*(*LOLA *looks nervously at* DOC. DOC *looks puzzled and a little sore.)*

MARIE. Bruce is coming! "Arriving tomorrow 5:00 P.M. CST, Flight 22, Love, Bruce." When did the telegram come?
DOC. So it came an hour ago. *(To kitchen.)*
LOLA. *(Nervously)* Isn't it nice I got the house all cleaned? Marie, you bring Bruce to dinner with us tomorrow night. It'll be a sort of wedding present.
MARIE. *(Right)* That would be wonderful, Mrs. Delaney, but I don't want you to go to any trouble.
LOLA. No trouble at all. Now I insist. *(Front DOORBELL rings.)* That must be Turk.
MARIE. *(Whispers)* Don't tell *him. (Goes to door.* LOLA *scampers to kitchen.)* Hi, Turk. Come on in.
TURK. *(Entering. Stalks her)* Hi. *(Looks around to see if anyone is present, then takes her in his arms and starts to kiss her.)*
LOLA. I'm sorry, Doc. I'm sorry about the telegram.
DOC. Baby, people don't do things like that. Don't you understand? *Nice* people don't.

MARIE. Stop it!
TURK. What's the matter?
MARIE. They're in the kitchen. *(Goes into bedroom.)*

(TURK sits with book.)

Doc. Why didn't you give it to her when it came?
LOLA. Well, Doc, Turk was posing for Marie this morning, and I couldn't give it to her while he was here.

(TURK listens at door.)

Doc. Well, it just isn't nice to open other people's mail.

(TURK crosses up to MARIE'S door.)

LOLA. I guess I'm not nice, then. That what you mean?
MARIE. Turk, will you get away from that door?
      (LIGHT Q #3. Chandalier out. Areas down.)
Doc. No, Baby, but—
LOLA. I don't see any harm in it, Doc. I steamed it open and sealed it back. (TURK *at switch in living room.)* She'll never know the difference. I don't see any harm in that, Doc.
Doc. *(Gives up)* OK, Baby, if you don't see any harm in it, I guess I can't explain it. *(Starts getting ready to go.)*
LOLA. I'm sorry, Doc. Honest, I'll never do it again. Will you forgive me?
Doc. *(Giving her a peck of a kiss)* I forgive you.
MARIE. *(Comes back with book)* Let's look like we're studying.   *(LIGHT Q #4. Bedroom out.)*
TURK. Biology? Hot dog!
LOLA. *(After MARIE leaves her room)* Now I feel better. Do you have to go now?

(TURK sits by MARIE on aavenport.)

Doc. Yah.

Lola. Before you go why don't you show your tricks to Marie.

Doc. *(Reluctantly)* Not now.

Lola. *(To door up Right)* Oh, please do. They'd be crazy about them.

Doc. *(With pride)* O.K. *(Preens himself a little)* If you think they'd enjoy them— (Lola, *starting to living room, stops suddenly upon seeing* Marie *and* Turk *spooning behind a book. A broad, pleased smile breaks on her face and she stands silently watching.* Doc, *at sink)* Well—what's the matter, Baby?

Lola. *(Soft voice)* Oh—nothing—nothing—Doc.

Doc. Well, do you want me to show 'em my tricks or don't you?

Lola. *(Coming back to Center of kitchen; in a secretive voice with a little giggle)* I guess they wouldn't be interested now.

Doc. *(With injured pride. A little sore)* Oh, very well.

Lola. Come and look, Daddy.

Doc. *(Shocked and angry)* NO!

Lola. Just one little look. They're just kids, Daddy. It's sweet. *(Drags him by arm.)*

Doc. *(Jerking loose)* Stop it, Baby. I won't do it. It's not decent to snoop around spying on people like that. It's cheap and mischievous and mean.

Lola. *(This had never occurred to her)* Is it?

Doc. Of course it is.

Lola. I don't spy on Marie and Turk to be mischievous and mean.

Doc. Then why *do* you do it?

Lola. You watch young people make love in the movies, don't you, Doc? There's nothing wrong with that. And I *know* Marie and I like her, and Turk's nice, too. They're both so young and pretty. Why shouldn't I watch them?

Doc. I give up.

Lola. Well, why shouldn't I?

Doc. I don't know, Baby, but it's not nice.

(TURK *kisses* MARIE'S *ear.*)

LOLA. I think it's one of the nicest things I know.
(Plaintive.)

MARIE. Let's go out on the porch.

(They steal out.)

Doc. It's not right for Marie to do that, particularly
since Bruce is coming. We shouldn't allow it.

LOLA. Oh, they don't do any harm, Doc. I think it's
all right.

Doc. It's not all right. I don't know why you encourage that sort of thing.

LOLA. I don't encourage it.

Doc. You do, too. You like that fellow Turk. You
said so. And I say he's no good. Marie's sweet and in-
nocent; she doesn't understand guys like him. I think
I oughta run him outa the house.

LOLA. Daddy, you wouldn't do that.

Doc. *(Very heated)* Then you talk to her and tell her
how we feel.

LOLA. Hush, Daddy. They'll hear you.

Doc. I don't care if they do hear me.

LOLA. *(To* Doc *at stove)* Don't get upset, Daddy.
Bruce is coming and Turk won't be around any longer.
I promise you.

Doc. All right. I better go.

LOLA. I'll go with you, Doc. Just let me run up and
get a sweater. Now wait for me.

Doc. Hurry, Baby.

(LOLA *goes upstairs.* DOC *is at platform when he hears*
TURK *laugh on the porch. He goes down Left to
cabinet—sees whisky bottle. Reaches for it and
hears* MARIE *giggle. Turns away as* TURK *laughs
again. Turns back to the bottle and hears* LOLA'S
voice from upstairs. MARIE *and* TURK *return to*

living room. Turk *takes* Lola's *picture from shelf up Right.)*

Lola. I'll be there in a minute, Doc. *(Enters downstairs)* I'm all ready. (Doc *turns out kitchen LIGHTS and they go into living room.)* I'm walking Doc down to the bus. (Doc *sees* Turk *with* Lola's *picture. Takes it out of his hand, puts it on shelf up Right as* Lola *leads him out.* Doc *is off.)* Come on, Dad, here's your hat. Then I'll go for a long walk in the moonlight. Have a good time. *(She exits.)*

Marie. 'Bye, Mrs. Delaney. *(Exits.)*

Turk. He hates my guts. *(To front door.)*

Marie. Oh, he does not. *(Follows* Turk, *blocks his exit in door.)*

Turk. Yes, he does. If you ask me, he's jealous.

Marie. Jealous?

Turk. I've always thought he had a crush on you.

Marie. Now, Turk, don't be silly. Doc is nice to me. It's just in a few little things he does, like fixing my breakfast, but he's nice to everyone.

Turk. He ever make a pass?

Marie. No. He'd never get fresh.

Turk. He better not.

Marie. Turk, don't be ridiculous. Doc's such a nice, quiet man; if he gets any fun out of running his fingers through my hair, why not?

Turk. He's got a wife of his own, hasn't he? Why doesn't he make a few passes at her?

Marie. Things like that are none of our business.

Turk. O.K. How about a snuggle, Lovely?

Marie. *(A little prim and businesslike)* No more for tonight, Turk. *(Crosses down Left.)*

Turk. Why's tonight different from any other night?

Marie. I think we should make it a rule, every once in a while, just to sit and talk. *(Starts to sit davenport—crosses to chair down Right.)*

Turk. *(Restless. Sits davenport)* O.K. What'll we talk about?

MARIE. Well—there's lotsa things.

TURK. O.K. Start in.

MARIE. A person doesn't start a conversation that way.

TURK. Start it any way you want to.

MARIE. Two people should have something to talk about, like politics or psychology or religion.

TURK. How 'bout sex?

MARIE. *(Rises; crosses Left)* Turk!

TURK. *(Chases her around davenport)* Have you read the Kinsey report, Miss Buckholder?

MARIE. I should say not.

TURK. How old were you when you had your first affair, Miss Buckholder?—and did you ever have relations with your grandfather?

MARIE. Turk, stop it.

TURK. You wanted to talk about something; I was only trying to please. Let's have a kiss.

MARIE. Not tonight.

TURK. Who you savin' it up for?

MARIE. Don't talk that way.

TURK. *(Yawns—crosses to door)* Well, thanks, Miss Buckholder, for a nice evening. It's been a most enjoyable talk.

MARIE. *(To up Center. Anxious)* Turk, where are you going?

TURK. I guess I'm a man of action, Baby.

MARIE. Turk, don't go.

TURK. Why not? I'm not doin' any good here.

MARIE. Don't go.

TURK. *(Returns and she touches him. Sits davenport)* Now why didn't you think of this before? C'mon, let's get to work. *(They sit on davenport.)*

(LIGHT Q #6. Upstage areas down.)

MARIE. Oh Turk, this is all we ever do.

TURK. Are you complaining?

MARIE. *(Weakly)* —no.

TURK. Then what do you want to put on such a front for?

MARIE. —it's not a front.

(SOUND Q #9. Start other record and blend.)

TURK. What else is it? *(Mimicking)* Oh, no, Turk. Not tonight, Turk. I want to talk about philosophy, Turk. *(Himself again)* When all the time you know that if I went outa here without givin' you a good lovin' up you'd be sore as hell— Wouldn't you?

MARIE. *(She has to admit to herself it's true; she chuckles)* Oh—Turk—

TURK. It's true, isn't it?

MARIE. Maybe.

TURK. How about tonight, Lovely; going to be lonesome?

MARIE. Turk, you have the Spring Relays.

TURK. What of it? I can throw that old javelin any old time, *any* old time. C'mon, Baby, we've got by with it before, haven't we?

MARIE. I'm not so sure.

TURK. What do you mean?

MARIE. Sometimes I think Mrs. Delaney knows.

TURK. Well, bring her along.

MARIE. *(A pretense of being shocked)* Turk!

TURK. What makes you think so?

MARIE. Women just sense those things. She asks so many questions. *(WARN Curtain.)*

TURK. She ever *say* anything?

MARIE. No.

TURK. Now *you're* imagining things.

MARIE. Maybe.

TURK. Well, stop it.

MARIE. *(Rises—crosses Right)* O.K.

TURK. *(Rises—follows MARIE)* Honey, I know I talk awful rough around you at times; I never was a very gentlemanly bastard, but you really don't mind it —do you? *((She only smiles mischievously.))* Anyway, you know I'm nuts about you.

MARIE. *(Smug)* Are you?

(Now they engage in a little rough-house, he cuffing her like an affectionate bear, she responding with "Stop it," "Turk, that hurt," etc. And she slaps him playfully. Then they laugh together at their own pretense. Now LOLA *enters the back way very quietly, tiptoeing through the dark kitchen, standing by the doorway where she can peek at them. There is a quiet, satisfied smile on her face. She watches every move they make, alertly.)*

TURK. Now, Miss Buckholder, what is your opinion of the psychodynamic pressure of living in the atomic age?

MARIE. *(Playfully)* Turk, don't make fun of me.

TURK. Tonight?

MARIE. *(Her eyes dance as she puts him off just a little longer)* —well.

TURK. Tonight will never come again. *(This is true. She smiles.)* O.K.?

MARIE. Tonight will never come again— O.K. *(They embrace and start to dance.)* Let's go out somewhere first and have a few beers. We can't came back till they're asleep.

*(*TURK *turns out lamp. LIGHT Q #7. Areas down.)*

TURK. O.K.

(They dance slowly out the door. Then LOLA *moves quietly into the living room and out onto the porch. There she can be heard calling plaintively in a lost voice.)*

LOLA. Little Sheba—come back— Come back, Little Sheba. Come back.

CURTAIN

INTERMISSION

ACT TWO

Scene I

The next morning. Lola *and* Doc *are at breakfast again.* Lola *is rambling on while* Doc *sits meditatively, his head down, his face in his hands.*

Lola. *(In a light, humorous way, as though the faults of youth were as blameless as the uncontrollable actions of a puppy. Chuckles)* Then they danced for a while and went out together, arm in arm—

Doc. *(Left of table. Very nervous and tense)* I don't wanta hear any more about it, Baby.

Lola. What's the matter, Docky?

Doc. Nothing.

Lola. You look like you didn't feel very good.

Doc. I didn't sleep well last night.

Lola. You didn't take any of those sleeping pills, did you?

Doc. No.

Lola. Well, don't. The doctors say they're terrible for you.

Doc. I'll feel better after awhile.

Lola. Of course you will.

Doc. What time did Marie come in last night?

Lola. I don't know, Doc. I went to bed early and went right to sleep. Why?

Doc. Oh—nothing.

Lola. You musta slept if you didn't hear her.

Doc. I heard her; it was after midnight.

Lola. Then what did you ask me for?

Doc. I wasn't sure it was her.

Lola. What do you mean?

48

Doc. I thought I heard a man's voice.

Lola. Turk probably brought her inside the door.

Doc. *(Troubled)* I thought I heard someone laughing. A man's laugh— I guess I was just hearing things.

Lola. *(Rises, to sink)* Say your prayer?

Doc. *(Gets up)* Yes.

Lola. Kiss me 'bye. *(He leans over and kisses her, then puts on his coat and starts to leave.)* Do you think you could get home a little early? I want you to help me entertain Bruce. Marie said he'd be here about 5 :30. I'm going to have a lovely dinner: stuffed pork chops, twice-baked potatoes, and asparagus, and for dessert a big chocolate cake and maybe ice cream—

Doc. Sounds fine.

Lola. So you get home and help me.

Doc. O.K. *(Doc leaves kitchen and goes into living room. Again on the chair down Right is* Marie's *scarf. He picks it up as before and fondles it. Then there is the sound of* Turk's *laughter, soft and barely audible. It sounds like the laugh of a sated Bacchus. Doc's body stiffens. It is a sickening fact he must face and it has been revealed to him in its ugliest light. The lyrical grace, the spiritual ideal of Ave Maria is shattered. He has been fighting the truth, maybe suspecting all along that he was deceiving himself. Now he looks as though he might vomit. All his blind confusion is inside him. With an immobile expression of blankness of his face, he stumbles into the table above the davenport.)*

Lola. *(Still in kitchen)* Haven't you gone yet, Docky?

Doc. *(Dazed)* No—no, Baby.

Lola. *(Coming in doorway)* Anything the matter?

Doc. No—no. I'm all right now. *(To Right, drops scarf, takes hat. He has managed to sound perfectly natural. He braces himself and goes out.)*

*(*Lola *stands a moment, looking after him with a little curiosity. Then* Mrs. Coffman *enters, sticks her head in back door.)*

MRS. COFFMAN. Anybody home?

LOLA. *(On platform)* 'Morning, Mrs. Coffman.

MRS. COFFMAN. *(Inspecting the kitchen's new look)*
So this is what you've been up to, Mrs. Delaney.

LOLA. *(Proud)* Yes, I been busy.

(MARIE'S *door opens and closes.* MARIE *sticks her head
out of her bedroom door to see if the coast is
clear, then sticks her head back in again to whis-
per to* TURK *that he can leave without being ob-
served.*)

MRS. COFFMAN. Busy? Good Lord, I never seen
such activity. What got into you, Lady?

LOLA. Company tonight. I thought I'd fix things up a
little.

MRS. COFFMAN. You mean you done all this in one
day?

LOLA. *(With simple pride)* I said I been busy.

MRS. COFFMAN. Dear God, you done your spring
housecleaning all in one day.

(TURK *appears in living room.*)

LOLA. *(Appreciating this)* I fixed up the living room
a little, too.

MRS. COFFMAN. I must see it. *(Goes into living room.*
TURK *apprehends her and ducks back into* MARIE'S
room, shutting the door behind himself and MARIE.) I
declare! Overnight you turn the place into something
really swanky.

LOLA. Yes, and I bought a few new things, too.

MRS. COFFMAN. Neat as a pin, and so warm and
cozy. *(Sits Right)* I take my hat off to you, Mrs.
Delaney. I didn't know you had it in you. All these
years, now, I been sayin' to myself, "That Mrs.
Delaney is a good for nothing—sits around the house
all day, and never so much as shakes a dust mop." I
guess it just shows, we never really know what people
are like.

LOLA. I still got some coffee, Mrs. Coffman.

MRS. COFFMAN. Not now, Mrs. Delaney. Seeing your house so clean makes me feel ashamed. I gotta get home and get to work. *(To kitchen.)*

LOLA. *(Follows)* I hafta get busy, too. I got to get out all the silver and china. I like to set the table early, so I can spend the rest of the day looking at it.

(BOTH *laugh.)*

MRS. COFFMAN. Good day, Mrs. Delaney. *(Exits.)*

(Hearing the screen door slam, MARIE guards the kitchen door and TURK slips out the front. But neither has counted on DOC's reappearance. After seeing that TURK is safe, MARIE blows a goodbye kiss to him and joins LOLA in the kitchen. But DOC is coming in the front door just as TURK starts to go out. There is a moment of blind embarrassment, during which DOC only looks stupefied and TURK, after mumbling an unintelligible apology, runs out. First DOC is mystified, trying to figure it all out. His face looks more and more troubled. Meanwhile, MARIE and LOLA are talking in kitchen.)

MARIE. Boo! *(Sneaking up behind LOLA at back porch.)*

LOLA. *(Jumping around)* Heavens! You scared me, Marie. You up already?

MARIE. Yah.

LOLA. This is Saturday. You could sleep as late as you wanted.

MARIE. I thought I'd get up early and help you. *(Pouring a cup of coffee.)*

LOLA. Honey, I'd sure appreciate it. You can put up the table in the living room, after you've had your breakfast. That's where we'll eat. Then you can help me set it.

(Doc *closes door.*)

MARIE. O.K.

LOLA. Want a sweet roll?

MARIE. I don't think so. Turk and I had so much beer last night. He got kinda tight.

LOLA. He shouldn't do that, Marie.

MARIE. *(Starts for living room)* Just keep the coffee hot for me. I'll want another cup in a minute. *(Stops on seeing Doc)* Why, Mr. Delaney! I thought you'd gone.

DOC. *(In his usual manner)* Good morning, Marie. *(But not looking at her.)*

MARIE. *(She immediately wonders)* Why—why—how long have you been here, Doc?

DOC. *(Sits down Right)* Just got here, just this minute.

LOLA. That you, Daddy? *(Comes in.)*

DOC. It's me.

LOLA. What are you doing back?

DOC. *(Crossing around couch)* I—I just thought I'd feel better—if I took a glass of soda water —

LOLA. I'm afraid you're not well, Daddy.

DOC. I'm all right. *(Starts for kitchen.)*

LOLA. *(Helping MARIE move table from behind davenport to Right Center)* The soda's on the drain board.

(Doc *goes to kitchen, fixes some soda, but apparently to be alone for a few minutes. He stands a moment, just thinking. Then he sits sipping the soda, as though he were trying to make up his mind about something.)*

(WARN Curtain. SOUND Q #1. LIGHTS.)

LOLA. Marie, would you help me move the table? It'd be nice now if we had a dining room, wouldn't it? But if we had a dining room, I guess we wouldn't have you, Marie. It was my idea to turn the dining room into a bedroom and rent it. I thought of lots of things

to do for extra money—a few years ago—when Doc
was so—so sick.

(They set up table. LOLA gets cloth from cabinet up Left.)

MARIE. This is a lovely tablecloth.

LOLA. Irish linen. Doc's mother gave it to us when
we got married. She gave us all our silver and china,
too. The china's Havelin. I'm so proud of it. It's the
most valuable possession we own. I just washed it—
Will you help me bring it in? *(Getting china from
kitchen)* Doc was sortuva Mama's boy. He was an
only child and his mother thought the sun rose and set
in him. Didn't she, Docky? She brought Doc up like
a real gentleman.

MARIE. Where are the napkins?

LOLA. Oh, I forgot them. They're so nice I keep
them in my bureau drawer with my handkerchiefs.
Come upstairs and we'll get them.

*(LOLA and MARIE go upstairs. Then, Doc listens to be
sure LOLA and MARIE are upstairs, looks cautiously
at the whiskey bottle on cabinet shelf, but manages to resist several times. Finally he gives in to
temptation, grabs bottle off shelf, then starts won-
dering how to get past LOLA with it. Finally, it
occurs to him to wrap it inside his trench coat,
which he gets from closet and carries it over his
arm. LOLA and MARIE are heard upstairs and they
return to the living room and continue setting table
as DOC enters from kitchen on his way out.)*

LOLA. *(Coming downstairs)* Did you ever notice
how nice he keeps his fingernails? Not many men think
of things like that. And he used to take his mother to
church every Sunday.

MARIE. *(At table)* Oh, Doc's a real gentleman.

LOLA. Treats women like they were all beautiful

angels. We went together a whole year before he even kissed me. (Doc *comes through the living room with coat and bottle, going to front door.*) On your way back to the office now, Docky?

Doc. *(His back to them)* Yes.

Lola. *(Right end of table)* Aren't you going to kiss me goodbye before you go, Daddy? *(She goes to him and kisses him.* Marie *catches Doc's eye and smiles. Then she exits to her room, leaving door open)* Get home early as you can. I'll need you. We gotta give Bruce a royal welcome.

Doc. Yes, Baby.

Lola. Feeling all right?

Doc. Yes.

Lola. *(In doorway. He is on porch.)* Take care of yourself.

Doc. *(Toneless voice)* Goodbye. *(He goes.)*

Lola. *(Coming back to table with pleased expression, which changes to a puzzled look. Calls to* Marie) Now that's funny. Why did Doc take his raincoat? It's a beautiful day. There isn't a cloud in sight.

> *(Medium fast Curtain. As Curtain starts, SOUND Q #1.)*

CURTAIN

ACT TWO

Scene II

Both chandeliers on. Floor lamps on. Late evening light. Evening light on stage. Front and back doors closed. Sound out. Foots out.

It is now 5:30. The scene is the same as the preceding except that more finishing touches have been added and the Two Women, *still primping the*

table, lighting the tapers, are dressed in their best.
LOLA *is arranging the centerpiece.*

LOLA. *(Above table, fixing flowers)* I just love lilacs,
don't you, Marie? *(Takes one and studies it)* Mrs.
Coffman was nice; she let me have all I wanted. *(Looks
at it very closely)* Aren't they pretty? And they smell
so sweet. I think they're the nicest flower there is.

MARIE. *(Left of table)* They don't last long.

LOLA. *(Respectfully)* No. Just a few days. Mrs.
Coffman's started blooming just day before yesterday.

MARIE. By the first of the week they'll all be gone.

LOLA. Vanish—they'll vanish into thin air. *(Gayer
now)* Here, Honey, we have them to spare *now*. Put
this in your hair. There. (MARIE *does. Crossing to
kitchen)* Mrs. Coffman's been so nice lately. I didn't
use to like her. Now where could Doc be? He
didn't even come home for lunch.

MARIE. *(Gets two chairs from bedroom)* Mrs.
Delaney, you're a peach to go to all this trouble.

LOLA. *(Gets salt and pepper)* Shoot, I'm gettin'
more fun out of it than you are. Do you think Bruce is
going to like us?

MARIE. If he doesn't, I'll never speak to him again.

LOLA. *(Right of table. Eagerly)* I'm just dying to
meet him. But I feel sorta bad I never got to do anything nice for Turk.

MARIE. *(Carefully prying)* Did—Doc ever say anything to you about Turk—and me?

LOLA. About Turk and you? No, Honey. Why?

MARIE. I just wondered.

LOLA. What if Bruce finds out that you've been
going with someone else?

MARIE. Bruce and I had a very businesslike understanding before I left for school that we weren't going
to sit around lonely just because we were separated.

LOLA. Aren't you being kind of mean to Turk?

MARIE. I don't think so.

LOLA. How's he going to feel when Bruce comes?

MARIE. He may be sore for a little while, but he has plenty of other girls. He'll get over it.

LOLA. Won't he feel bad?

MARIE. He's had his eye on a pretty little Spanish girl in his history class for a long time. I like Turk, but he's not the marrying kind. *(To mirror on whatnot up Right.)*

LOLA. No! Really? (LOLA, *with a look of sad wonder on her face, sits Right arm of couch. It's been a serious disillusionment.)*

MARIE. What's the matter? *(Crosses to LOLA.)*

LOLA. I—I just felt kinda tired.

(Sharp buzzing of DOORBELL. MARIE runs to answer it.)

MARIE. That must be Bruce. *(She skips to the mirror again, then to door)* Bruce!

BRUCE. *(Entering)* How are you, Sweetheart?

MARIE. Wonderful.

BRUCE. Did you get my wire?

MARIE. Sure.

BRUCE. You're looking swell.

MARIE. Thanks. What took you so long to get here?

BRUCE. Well, Honey, I had to go to my hotel and take a bath.

MARIE. Bruce, this is Mrs. Delaney.

BRUCE. *(Now he gets the cozy quality out of his voice)* How do you do, Ma'am?

LOLA. How d'ya do?

BRUCE. Marie has said some very nice things about you in her letters.

MARIE. Mrs. Delaney has fixed the grandest dinner for us.

BRUCE. Now that was to be my treat. I have a big expense account now, Honey. I thought we could all go down to the hotel and have dinner there, and celebrate first with a few cocktails.

LOLA. Oh, we can have cocktails, too. Excuse me just

a minute. *(She hurries to the kitchen and starts look-ing for the whiskey.)*

(BRUCE *kisses* MARIE. *Then she whispers:*)

MARIE. Now, Bruce, she's been working on this dinner all day. She even cleaned the house for you.
BRUCE. Did she?
MARIE. *(Crossing up stage Left of table)* And Doc's joining us. You'll like Doc.
BRUCE. *(Follows up Right side of table)* Honey, are we going to have to stay here the whole evening?
MARIE. We just can't eat and run right away. We'll get away as soon as we can.
BRUCE. I hope so. I got the raise, Sweetheart. They're giving me new territory.

(LOLA *is frantic in the kitchen, having found the bottle missing. She hurries back into the living room.)*

LOLA. You kids are going to have to entertain your-selves a while cause I'm going to be busy in the kitchen. Why don't you turn on the radio, Marie? Get some dance music. I'll shut the door so—so I won't disturb you. (LOLA *does so. Then goes to the telephone.)*
MARIE. Come and see my room, Bruce. I've fixed it up just darling. And I've got your picture in the pret-tiest frame right on my dresser.

(*They exit and their voices are heard from the bedroom while* LOLA *is telephoning.)*

LOLA. *(At the telephone)* This is Mrs. Delaney. Is— Doc there? Well, then, is Ed Anderson there? Well, would you give me Ed Anderson's telephone number? You see, he sponsored Doc into the club and helped him—you know—and—and I was a little worried to-night— Oh, thanks. Yes, I've got it. *(She writes down number)* Could you have Ed Anderson call me if he comes in? Thank you. *(She hangs up. On her face is a dismal expression of fear, anxiety and doubt. She searches flour bin, icebox, closet. Then she goes into the living room, calling to* MARIE *and* BRUCE *as she comes)* I—I guess we'll go ahead without Doc, Marie.

MARIE. *(Enters from her room)* What's the matter with Doc, Mrs. Delaney?

LOLA. Well—he got held up at the office—just one of those things, you know. It's too bad. It would have to happen when I needed him most.

MARIE. Sure you don't need any help?

LOLA. Huh? Oh, no. I'll make out. Everything's ready. I tell you what I'm going to do. Three's a crowd, so I'm going to be the butler and serve the dinner to you two young lovebirds— *(The TELEPHONE rings.* MARIE *goes into bedroom.)* Pardon me—pardon me just a minute. *(She rushes to telephone, closing the door behind her)* Hello? Ed? Have you seen Doc? He went out this morning and hasn't come back. We're having company for dinner and he was supposed to be home early— That's not all. This time we've had a quart of whiskey in the kitchen and Doc's never gone near it. I went to get it tonight. I was going to serve some cocktails. It was *gone.* Yes, I saw it there yesterday. No, I don't think so —He said this morning he had an upset stomach but— Oh would you?—Thank you, Mr. Anderson.

Thank you a million times. And you let me know when you find out anything. Yes, I'll be here. Yes. *(Hangs up and crosses back to living room)* Well, I guess we're all ready.

(Their voices continue in bedroom.)

BRUCE. Aren't you going to look at your present?

MARIE. Oh, sure; let's get some scissors.

MARIE. *(Enters with* BRUCE) Mrs. Delaney, we think you should eat with us.

LOLA. Oh, no, Honey. I'm not very hungry. Besides, this is the first time you've been together in months and I think you should be alone. Marie, why don't you light the candles, then we'll have just the right atmosphere. *(She goes into kitchen, gets tomato juice glasses from ice box while* BRUCE *lights the candles.)*

BRUCE. Do we have to eat by candlelight? I won't be able to see.

LOLA. *(Returns)* Now, Bruce, you sit here. *(He and* MARIE *sit.)* Isn't that going to be cozy? Dinner for two. Sorry we won't have time for cocktails. Let's have a little music. *(SOUND Q #2. She turns on the radio and a Viennese waltz swells up as the Curtain falls, with* LOLA *looking at the young people eating.)*

CURTAIN

ACT TWO

SCENE III

Front door closed. Bedroom door closed. Kitchen to living room door open. Back door open.

Funeral atmosphere. It is about 5:30 the next morning. The sky is just beginning to get light outside. While inside the room the shadows still cling heavily to the corners. The remains of last night's dinner clutter the table in the living room. The candles have guttered down to stubs amid the dirty dinner plates, and the lilacs in the centerpiece have wilted. LOLA *is sprawled on the davenport, sleeping. Slowly she awakens and regards the morning light. She gets up and looks about strangely, beginning to show despair for the situation she is in. She wears the same spiffy dress she had on the night before, but it is wrinkled now, and her marcelled coiffure is awry. One silk stocking has twisted loose and falls around her ankle. When she is sufficiently awake to realize her situa-*

tion, she rushes to the telephone and dials a number.

LOLA. *(At telephone. She sounds frantic)* Mr. Anderson? Mr. Anderson, this is Mrs. Delaney again. I'm sorry to call you so early, but I just *had* to— Did you find Doc?—No, he's not home yet. I don't suppose he'll come home till he's drunk all he can hold and wants to sleep— I don't know what else to think, Mr. Anderson. I'm scared, Mr. Anderson. I'm awful scared. Will you come right over?—Thanks, Mr. Anderson. *(Hangs up and goes to kitchen to make coffee. She finds some left from the night before, so turns on the fire to warm it up. She wanders around vaguely, trying to get her thoughts in order, jumping at every sound. Pours herself a cup of coffee, then takes it to living room, sits down Right and sips it. LIGHT Q A. Very quietly Doc enters through the back way into the kitchen. He carries a big bottle of whiskey, which he carefully places back in the cabinet, not making a sound—hangs up overcoat, then puts suitcoat on back of chair. Starts to go upstairs. But LOLA speaks)* Doc? That you, Doc?

(Then Doc quietly walks in from kitchen. He is staggering drunk, but he is managing for a few minutes to appear as though he were perfectly sober and nothing had happened. His steps, however, are not too sure and his eyes are like blurred ink pots. LOLA is too frightened to talk. Her mouth is gaping and she is breathless with fear.)

(LIGHT Q #1. General brightening.)

DOC. Good morning, Honey.

LOLA. Doc! You all right?

DOC. *(Crossing down Right by chair)* The morning paper here? I wanta see the morning paper.

LOLA. Doc, we don't get a morning paper. *You* know that.

DOC. *(Sits down Right)* Oh, then I suppose I'm drunk or something. That what you're trying to say?

LOLA. No, Doc—

DOC. Then give me the morning paper.

LOLA. *(Scampering to get last night's paper from table Left)* Sure, Doc. Here it is. Now you just sit there and be quiet.

DOC. *(Resistance rising)* Why shouldn't I be quiet?

LOLA. Nothin', Doc—

DOC. *(Has trouble unfolding paper. He places it before his face in order not to be seen. But he is too blind even to see. Mockingly)* Nothing, Doc.

LOLA. *(Cautiously, after a few minute's silence)* Doc, are you all right?

DOC. Of course I'm all right. Why should I be all right?

LOLA. Where you been?

DOC. What's it your business where I been? I been to London to see the Queen. What do you think of that? *(Apparently she doesn't know what to think of it.)* Just let me alone. That's all I ask. I'm all right.

LOLA. *(Sits Right end of davenport. Simpering)* Doc, what made you do it? You said you'd be home last night—'cause we were having company. Bruce was here and I had a big dinner fixed—and you never came. What was the matter, Doc?

DOC. *(Mockingly)* We had a big dinner for *Bruce*.

LOLA. Doc, it was for you, too.

DOC. Well—I don't want it.

LOLA. Don't get mad, Doc.

DOC. *(Threateningly. Rises, crosses up Center)* Where's Marie?

LOLA. I don't know, Doc. She didn't come in last night. She was out with Bruce.

DOC. *(Back to audience)* I suppose you tucked them in bed together and peeked through the keyhole and applauded.

LOLA. *(Sickened)* Doc, don't talk that way. Bruce is a nice boy. They're gonna get married.

DOC. He probably *has* to marry her, the poor bastard.

Just 'cause she's pretty and he got amorous one day—
Just like I had to marry *you*.

LOLA. Oh, Doc!

DOC. You and Marie are both a couple of sluts.

LOLA. *(Rises; crosses Right)* Doc, please don't talk
like that.

DOC. What are you good for? You can't even get up
in the morning and cook my breakfast.

LOLA. *(Mumbling)* I will, Doc. I will after this.

DOC. You won't even sweep the floors till some bozo
comes along to make love to Marie, and then you fix
things up like Buckingham Palace or a Chinese whore-
house with perfume on the lampbulbs, and flowers, and
the gold-trimmed china *my mother* gave us. We're not
going to use these any more. My mother didn't buy
those dishes for whores to eat off of. *(Jerks the cloth
off the table, sending the dishes rattling to the floor.)*

LOLA. *(Breaking Left)* Doc! Look what you done.

DOC. Look what I *did*, not *done*. I'm going to get me
a drink. *(To kitchen.)*

LOLA. *(Follows to platform)* Oh no, Doc! You know
what it does to you!

DOC. You're damn right I know what it does to me.
It makes me willing to come home here and look at you,
you two-ton old heifer. *(Gets bottle. Takes a long swallow)* There! And pretty soon I'm going to have another, then another.

LOLA. *(With dread)* Oh, Doc! (LOLA *takes phone.
DOC sees this, rushes for the butcher-knife in kitchen
cabinet drawer. Not finding it, he gets a hatchet from
the back porch.)* Mr. Anderson? Come quick, Mr. Anderson. He's back. He's *back!* He's got a hatchet!

DOC. God damn you! Get away from that telephone.
*(He chases her into living room, where she gets the
davenport between them;* LOLA *downstage,* DOC *up.)*
That's right, phone! Tell the world I'm drunk. Tell the
whole damn world. Scream your head off, you fat slut.
Holler till all the neighbors think I'm beatin' hell outuv
you. Where's Bruce now—under Marie's bed? You got

all fresh and pretty for him, didn't you? Combed your hair for once— You even washed the back of your neck, and put on a girdle. You were willing to harness all that fat into one bundle.

LOLA. *(About to faint under the weight of the crushing accusation)* Doc, don't say any more— I'd rather you hit me with an axe, Doc— Honest I would. But I can't stand to hear you talk like that.

DOC. I oughta hack off all that fat, and then wait for Marie and chop off those pretty ankles she's always dancing around on—then start lookin' for Turk and fix him too.

LOLA. Daddy, you're talking crazy!

DOC. *(Moves to above Right end of davenport)* I'm making sense for the first time in my life. You didn't know I knew about it, did you? But I saw him coming outa there. I saw him. You knew about it all the time and thought you were hidin' something—

LOLA. *(To up Center of davenport)* Daddy, I didn't know anything about it at all. Honest, Daddy.

DOC. Then *you're* the one that's crazy, if you think I didn't know. You were running a regular house, weren't you? It's probably been going on for years, ever since we were married. *(He lunges for her. She breaks for kitchen. They struggle in front of sink.)*

LOLA. Doc, it's not so; it's not so. You gotta believe me, Doc.

DOC. You're lyin'. But none a that's gonna happen any more. I'm gonna fix you now, once and for all—

LOLA. Doc—don't do that to me. (LOLA, *in a frenzy of fear, clutches him around the neck, holding arm with axe by his side)* Remember, Doc. It's *me*, Lola! You said I was the prettiest girl you ever saw. Remember, Doc! It's me! Lola!

DOC. *(The memory has overpowered him. He collapses, slowly mumbling)* Lola—my pretty Lola.

(He passes out on the floor. LOLA *stands, now, as*

though in a trance. Quietly MRS. COFFMAN *comes creeping in through the back way.)*

(*SOUND Q #3: Airplane O—1¼—O.*)

MRS. COFFMAN. *(Calling softly)* Mrs. Delaney! (LOLA *doesn't even hear.* MRS. COFFMAN *comes on in)* Mrs. Delaney!—Here you are, Lady. I heard screaming and I was frightened for you.

LOLA. I—I'll be all right—some men are comin' pretty soon; everything'll be all right. *(Sits Left of table.)*

MRS. COFFMAN. *(Crossing to* LOLA*)* I'll stay until they get here.

LOLA. *(Feeling a sudden need)* Would you—would you *please,* Mrs. Coffman? *(Breaks into sobs.)*

(*LIGHT Q #2. Areas up.*)

MRS. COFFMAN. Of course, Lady. *(Regarding* DOC*)* The Doctor got "sick" again?

LOLA. *(Mumbling)* Some men—'ll be here pretty soon—

MRS. COFFMAN. I'll try to straighten things up before they get here—

(She rights chair, hangs up telephone and picks up the axe, which she is holding when ED ANDERSON *and* ELMO HUSTON *enter front door unannounced. They are experienced AA's. Neatly dressed businessmen approaching middle-age.)*

ED. Pardon us for walking right in, Mrs. Delaney, but I didn't want to waste a second. *(To kitchen. Kneels at* DOC.)

LOLA. *(Weakly)* —it's all right—

(Both MEN *observe* DOC *on the floor, and their expressions hold understanding mixed with a feeling of irony. There is even a slight smile of irony on* ED's *face. They have developed the surgeon's objectivity.)*

ED. Where is the hatchet? *(To* ELMO, *as though appraising* Doc's *condition)* What do you think, Elmo?

ELMO. *(To down Left Center)* We can't leave him here if he's gonna play around with hatchets.

ED. Give me a hand, Elmo. We'll get him to sit up and then try to talk some sense into him. *(They struggle with the lumpy body,* Doc *grunting his resistance.)* Come on, Doc, old boy. It's Ed and Elmo. We're going to take care of you.

(They seat him Center at table.)

Doc. *(Through a thick fog)* Lemme alone.

ED. Wake up. We're taking you away from here.

Doc. Lemme 'lone, God damn it. *(Falls forward—head on table.)*

ELMO. *(To* MRS. COFFMAN) Is there any coffee?

MRS. COFFMAN. I think so. I'll see. *(To stove with cup from drainboard. Lights fire under coffee, and waits for it to get heated.)*

ED. He's way beyond coffee.

ELMO. It'll help some. Get something hot into his stomach.

ED. —if we could get him to eat. How 'bout some hot food, Doc?

(Doc gestures and they don't push the matter.)

ELMO. City hospital, Ed?

ED. I guess that's what it will have to be.

LOLA. Where you going to take him?

(ELMO goes to telephone—speaks quietly to City Hospital.)

ED. Don't know. Wanta talk to him first. *(To Left of* Doc.)

MRS. COFFMAN. *(Coming with the coffee)* Here's the coffee.

ED. *(Taking cup)* Hold him, Elmo, while I make him swallow this.

ELMO. *(To Right of* Doc) Come on, Doc, drink your coffee.

DOC. *(He only blubbers. After the coffee is down)* Uh—what—what's goin' on here?

ED. It's me, Doc. Your old friend Ed. I got Elmo with me.

DOC. *(Twisting his face painfully)* Get out, both of you. Lemme 'lone.

ED. *(With certainty)* We're takin' you with us, Doc.

DOC. Hell you are. I'm all right. I just had a little slip. We all have slips—

ED. Sometimes, Doc, but we gotta get over 'em.

DOC. I'll be O.K. Just gimme a day to sober up. I'll be as good as new.

ED. Remember the last time, Doc? You said you'd be all right in the morning and we found you with a broken collar bone. Come on.

DOC. Boys, I'll be all right. Now lemme alone.

ED. How much has he had, Mrs. Delaney?

LOLA. I don't know. He had a quart when he left here yesterday and he didn't get home till now.

ED. He's probably been through a *couple* of quarts. He's been dry for a long time. It's going to hit him pretty hard. Yah, he'll be a pretty sick man for a few days. *(Louder to* Doc, *as though he were talking to a deaf man)* Wanta go to the City Hospital, Doc?

DOC. *(This has a sobering effect on him. He looks about him furtively for possible escape)* No—no, boys. Don't take me there. That's a torture chamber. No, Ed. You wouldn't do that to me.   *(LIGHT Q #3.)*

ED. They'll sober you up.

DOC. Ed, I been there; I've seen the place. That's where they take the crazy people. You can't do that to me, Ed.

ED. Well, *you're* crazy, aren't you? Goin' after your wife with a hatchet.

(They lift Doc to his feet. Doc looks with dismal pleading in his eyes at LOLA, who has her face in her hands.)

DOC. *(So plaintive, a sob in his voice)* Honey! Honey! (LOLA *can't look at him. Now* DOC *tries to make a getaway, bolting blindly into the living room before the* TWO MEN *catch him and hold him in front of table)* Honey, don't let 'em take me there. They'll believe *you.* Tell 'em you won't *let* me take a drink.

LOLA. Isn't there any place else you could take him?

ED. Private sanitariums cost a lotta dough.

LOLA. I got forty dollars in the kitchen.

ED. That won't be near enough.

DOC. I'll be at the meeting tomorrow night sober as you are now.

ED. *(To* LOLA*)* All the king's horses couldn't keep him from takin' another drink now, Mrs. Delaney. He got himself into this; he's gotta sweat it out.

DOC. I won't go to the City Hospital. That's where they take the crazy people. *(Stumbles into chair down Right.)*

ED. *(Using all his patience now)* Look, Doc. Elmo and I are your friends. You know that. Now if you don't come along peacefully, we're going to call the cops and you'll have to wear off this jag in the cooler. How'd you like that? (Doc *is as though stunned.)* The important thing is for you to get sober.

DOC. I don't wanta go.

ED. The City Hospital or the City Jail. Take your choice. We're not going to leave you here. Come on, Elmo.

(They grab hold of him.)

DOC. *(Has collected himself and now given in)* O.K. boys. Gimme another drink and I'll go.

LOLA. Oh no, Doc.

Ed. Might as well humor him, Ma'am. Another few drinks couldn't make much difference now.

(Mrs. Coffman *runs for bottle and glass in cabinet, comes right back with them, hands them to* Lola.)

Ed. O.K., Doc, we're goin' to give you a drink. Take a good one; it's gonna be your last for a long time to come. (Ed *takes the bottle, removes the cork and gives* Doc *a glass of whiskey.* Doc *takes his fill, straight, coming up once or twice for air. Then* Ed *takes the bottle from him and hands it to* Lola. *To* Lola) They'll keep him three or four days, Mrs. Delaney; then he'll be home again, good as new. (*Modestly*) I— I don't want to pry into personal affairs, Ma'am—but he'll need you then, pretty bad—

Lola. I know.
Ed. Come on, Doc. Let's go.

(Ed *has a hold of* Doc's *coat sleeve, trying to maneuver him. A faraway look is in* Doc's *eyes, a dazed look containing panic and fear. He gets to his feet.*)

Doc. (*Struggling to sound reasonable*) Just a minute, boys—
Ed. What's the matter?
Doc. I—I wanta glass of water.
Ed. You'll get a glass of water later. Come on.
Doc. (*Beginning to twist a little in* Ed's *grasp*) —a glass of water—that's all— (*One furious, quick twist of his body and he eludes* Ed.)
Ed. Quick, Elmo.

(Elmo *acts fast and they get* Doc *before he gets away. Then* Doc *struggles with all his might, kicking and screaming like a pampered child,* Ed *and* Elmo *holding him tightly up Right of table to usher him out.*)

Doc. *(As he is led out)* Don't let 'em take me there. Don't take me there. Stop them, somebody. Stop them. That's where they take the crazy people. Oh God, stop them, somebody. Stop them.

(LOLA *looks on blankly while* ED *and* ELMO *depart with* Doc. *Sits down Right. Now there are several moments of deep silence.)*

MRS. COFFMAN. *(Clears up. Very softly)* Is there anything more I can do for you now, Mrs. Delaney?
LOLA. I guess not.
MRS. COFFMAN. *(Puts a hand on* LOLA's *shoulder)* Get busy, Lady. Get busy and forget it.
LOLA. Yes—I'll get busy right away. Thanks, Mrs. Coffman.
MRS. COFFMAN. I better go. I've got to make breakfast for the children. If you want me for anything, let me know.   *(LIGHT Q #4.)*
LOLA. Yes—yes— Goodbye, Mrs. Coffman.

(MRS. COFFMAN *exits back door.* LOLA *is too exhausted to move from the big chair. At first she can't even cry; then the tears come slowly, softly. In a few moments* BRUCE *and* MARIE *enter, bright and merry.* LOLA *turns her head slightly to regard them as creatures from another planet.)*

MARIE. *(Springing into room)* Congratulate me, Mrs. Delaney. *(To down Right.* BRUCE *follows.)*
LOLA. Huh?
MARIE. We're going to be married.
LOLA. Married? *(It barely registers.)*
MARIE. *(Showing ring)* Here it is. My engagement ring.

(MARIE *and* BRUCE *are too engrossed in their cwn happiness to notice* LOLA's *stupor.)*

LOLA. That's lovely—lovely.
MARIE. We've had the most wonderful time. We

danced all night and then drove out to the lake and saw the sun rise.

LOLA. That's nice.

MARIE. We've made all our plans. I'm quitting school and flying back to Cincinnati with Bruce this afternoon. His mother has invited me to visit them before I go home. Isn't that wonderful?

LOLA. Yes—yes, indeed.

MARIE. Going to miss me?

LOLA. Yes, of course, Marie. We'll miss you very much— Uh—congratulations.

MARIE. Thanks, Mrs. Delaney. *(Crosses up to bedroom door)* Come on, Bruce, help me get my stuff.

MARIE. Mrs. Delaney, would you throw everything into a big box and send it to me at home? We haven't had breakfast yet. We're going down to the hotel and celebrate.

BRUCE. I'm sorry we're in such a hurry, but we've got a taxi waiting.

(They go into bedroom.)

LOLA. *(To telephone, dials)* Long Distance? I want to talk to Green Valley 223. Yes. This is Delmar 1887.

(She hangs up, crosses down. As she gets below table, MARIE comes from bedroom, followed by BRUCE, who carries suitcase.)   *(WARN Curtain.)*

MARIE. Mrs. Delaney, I sure hate to say goodbye to you. You've been so wonderful to me. But Bruce says I can come and visit you once in a while, didn't you, Bruce?

BRUCE. Sure thing.

LOLA. You're going?

MARIE. We're going downtown and have our breakfast, then do a little shopping and catch our plane. And thanks for everything, Mrs. Delaney.

BRUCE. It was very nice of you to have us to dinner.

LOLA. Dinner? Oh, don't mention it.

MARIE. *(Crossing to* LOLA) There isn't much time for goodbye now, but I just want you to know Bruce and I wish you the best of everything. You and Doc both. Tell Doc goodbye for me, will you, and remember, I think you're both a coupla peaches.

BRUCE. Hurry, Honey.

MARIE. 'Bye, Mrs. Delaney! *(She goes out door.)*

BRUCE. 'Bye, Mrs. Delaney. Thanks for being nice to my girl. *(He goes out and off porch with* MARIE.)

LOLA. *(Waves. The TELEPHONE rings. She goes to it quickly)* Hello. Hello, Mom. It's Lola, Mom. How are you? Mom, Doc's sick again. Do you think Dad would let me come home for a while? I'm awfully unhappy, Mom. Do you think—just till I made up my mind?—All right. No, I guess it wouldn't do any good for you to come here— I—I'll let you know what I decide to do. That's all, Mom. Thanks. Tell Daddy hello. *(She hangs up.)*

CURTAIN

ACT TWO

SCENE IV

It is morning, a week later. The house is neat again, as in Act One, Scene II. LOLA *is dusting in the living room as* MRS. COFFMAN *enters from back door.*

MRS. COFFMAN. Mrs. Delaney! Good morning, Mrs. Delaney.

LOLA. Come in, Mrs. Coffman.

MRS. COFFMAN. *(Coming in. Crossing to* LOLA) It's a fine day for the games. I've got a box lunch ready, and I'm taking all the kids to the Stadium. My boy's got a ticket for you, too. You better get dressed and come with us.

LOLA. Thanks, Mrs. Coffman, but I've got work to do.

MRS. COFFMAN. But it's such a big day. The Spring Relays— All the athletes from the colleges are supposed to be there.   *(SOUND Q #4: Band Music.)*

LOLA. Oh yes. You know that boy Turk who used to come here to see Marie—he's one of the big stars.

MRS. COFFMAN. Is that so? Come on—do. We've got a ticket for you—

LOLA. Oh no, I have to stay here and clean up the house. Doc may be coming home today. I talked to him on the phone. He wasn't sure what time they'd let him out, but I wanta have the place all nice for him.

MRS. COFFMAN. That's right. Well, I'll tell you all about it when I come home. Everybody and his brother will be there.

LOLA. Yes, do, and have a good time.

MRS. COFFMAN. 'Bye, Mrs. Delaney.

LOLA. 'Bye.

(MRS. COFFMAN *leaves, and* LOLA *goes into kitchen. The* MAILMAN *comes onto porch and leaves a letter, but* LOLA *doesn't even know he's there. Then the* MILKMAN *knocks on the back door.)*

LOLA. Come in.

MILKMAN. *(Entering with arm full of bottles, etc.)* I see you checked the list, Lady. You've got a lot of extras.

LOLA. Ya—I think my husband's coming home.

MILKMAN. *(He puts the supplies on table, then pulls out magazine)* Remember, I told you my picture was going to appear in *Strength and Health.* (*Showing her magazine)* Well, see that pile of muscles? That's me.

LOLA. *(Totally without enthusiasm)* My goodness. You got your picture in a magazine.

MILKMAN. Yes, Ma'am. See what it says about my chest development? For the greatest self-improvement in a three months' period.

LOLA. Goodness sakes. You'll be famous, won't you?
MILKMAN. If I keep busy on these bar-bells. I'm
working now for "muscular separation."
LOLA. That's nice.
MILKMAN. *(Cheerily)* Well, good day, Ma'am.
LOLA. You forgot your magazine.
MILKMAN. That's for you. *(Exits.)*

(LOLA puts away the supplies in the ice-box. Then Doc
*comes in the front door carrying the little suitcase
she previously packed for him. The band MUSIC
is very dim now, but the triumphant strains of
BOOLA BOOLA can be heard in the far distance.*
Doc *is himself again. His quiet manner, his serious demeanor, are the same as before.* LOLA *comes
to living room platform; is shocked by his sudden
appearance. She jumps and can't help showing her
fright.)*

LOLA. Docky!

(Without thinking, she assumes an attitude of fear.
Doc *observes this and it obviously pains him.)*

Doc. Good morning, Honey. *(Pause.)*
LOLA. *(On platform)* Are—are you all right, Doc?
                              (Fade out SOUND.)
Doc. Yes, I'm all right. *(An awkward pause. Then*
Doc *tries to reassure her)* Honest, I'm all right, Hon-
ey. Please don't stand there like that—like I was
gonna—gonna—
LOLA. *(Tries to relax)* I'm sorry, Doc.
Doc. *(Crosses down Left)* How you been?
LOLA. Oh, I been all right, Doc. Fine.
Doc. Any news?
LOLA. I told you about Marie—over the phone.
Doc. Yah.

(The distant band MUSIC has stopped.)

LOLA. He was a very nice boy, Doc. Very nice.

DOC. That's good. I hope they'll be happy.

LOLA. *(Trying to sound bright)* She said—maybe she'd come back and visit us sometime. That's what she *said*.

DOC. *(Pause)* It—it's good to be home.

LOLA. Is it, Daddy?

DOC. Yah. *(Beginning to choke up just a little. Sits on davenport.)*

LOLA. *(Crossing to Left of Doc on davenport)* Did everything go all right— I mean—did they treat you well and—

DOC. *(Now loses control of his feelings. Tears in his eyes, he all but lunges at her, gripping her arms, drilling his head into her bosom)* Honey, don't ever leave me. *Please* don't ever leave me. If you do, they'd have to keep me down at that place all the time. I don't know what I said to you or what I did. I can't remember hardly anything. But please forgive me—please— please— And I'll try to make everything up.

LOLA. *(There is surprise on her face and new contentment. She becomes almost angelic in demeanor. Tenderly she places a soft hand on his head)* Daddy! Why, of course I'll never leave you. *(A smile of satisfaction)* You're all I've got. You're all I ever had.

DOC. *(Collecting himself now. Very tenderly he kisses her. LOLA sits beside Doc)* I—I feel better— already. *(LIGHT Q #1.)*

LOLA. *(Almost gay)* So do I. Have you had your breakfast?

DOC. No. The food there was terrible. When they told me I could go this morning, I decided to wait and fix myself breakfast here.

LOLA. *(Rises, crosses up Left of davenport. Happily)* Come on out in the kitchen and I'll get you a nice, big breakfast. I'll scramble some eggs and— You see I've got the place all cleaned up just the way you like it. *(Doc goes to kitchen.)* Now you sit down here and I'll get your fruit juice. *(He sits and she gets fruit juice from refrigerator.)* I've got bacon this morning, too. My, it's expensive now. And I'll light the oven and make you some toast, and here's some orange marmalade, and—

Doc. *(With a new feeling of control)* Fruit juice. I'll need lots of it for a while. The doctor said it would restore the vitamins. You see, that damn whiskey kills all the vitamins in your system, eats up all the sugar in your kidneys. They came around every morning and shot vitamins in my arm. Oh, it didn't hurt. And the doctor told me to drink a quart of fruit juice every day. And you better get some candy bars for me at the grocery this morning. Doctor said to eat lots of candy, try to replace the sugar.

Lola. I'll do that, Doc. Here's another glass of this pineapple juice now. I'll get some candy bars first thing.

Doc. The doctor said I should have a hobby. Said I should go out more. That's all that's wrong with me. I thought maybe I'd go hunting once in a while.

Lola. Yes, Doc. And bring home lots of good things to eat.

Doc. I'll get a big bird dog, too. Would you like a sad-looking old bird dog around the house?

Lola. Of course I would. *(All her life and energy have been restored)* You know what, Doc? I had another dream last night.   *(WARN Curtain.)*

Doc. About Little Sheba?

Lola. Oh, it was about everyone and everything. *(In a raptured tone. She gets bacon from ice box and starts to cook it)* Marie and I were going to the Olympics back in our old High School Stadium. There were thousands of people there. There was Turk out in the center of the field throwing the javelin. Every time he'd throw it, the crowd would roar—and you know who the man in charge was? It was my father. Isn't that funny?—but Turk kept changing into someone else all the time. And then my father disqualified him. So he had to sit on the sidelines—and guess who

took his place, Daddy? You! You came trotting out
there on the field just as big as you please—

Doc. *(Smilingly)* How did I do, Baby?

LOLA. Fine. You picked the javelin up real careful,
like it was awful heavy. But you threw it, Daddy, clear,
clear up into the sky. And it never came down again.
(Doc looks very pleased with himself. LOLA *goes on)*
Then it started to rain. And I couldn't find Little Sheba.
I almost went crazy looking for her and there were so
many people I didn't even know where to look. And
you were waiting to take me home. And we walked and
walked through the slush and mud, and people were
hurrying all around us and—and— *(Leaves stove and
sits. Sentimental tears come to her eyes)* But this part
is sad, Daddy. All of a sudden I saw Little Sheba—she
was lying in the middle of the field—dead— It made
me cry, Doc. No one paid any attention— I cried and
cried. It made me feel so bad, Doc. That sweet little
puppy—her curly white fur all smeared with mud, and
no one to stop and take care of her—

Doc. Why couldn't *you?*

LOLA. I wanted to, but you wouldn't let me. You kept
saying, "We can't stay here, Honey; we gotta go on.
We gotta go on." *(Pause)* Now, isn't that strange?

Doc. Dreams are funny.

LOLA. I don't think Little Sheba's ever coming back,
Doc. I'm not going to call her any more.

(CHEERS.)

Doc. Not much point in it, Baby. I guess she's gone
for good.

LOLA. I'll fix your eggs.

*(She gets up, embraces Doc, and goes to stove. Doc
remains at table sipping his fruit juice. The
Curtain comes slowly down—*

THE END

COME BACK, LITTLE SHEBA

STAGE MANAGER'S WORKING PLOT

2 :00
8 :00 Call half hour. Check on Cast. Observe setting; properties, side props, horn, and light wall switches.

2 :20
8 :20 Call 15 min. Final check of cast.

2 :30
8 :30 Call 5 min.

2 :35
8 :35 Call Overture, Places first act. Start orchestra. Check lights with electrician.

2 :39
8 :39 Dim house to half, hold. for 30 seconds, cue orchestra to stop, then dim out.

2 :40
8 :40 Curtain up.

ACT ONE, Scene I

During Act observe people ready for all entrances.

CUE: *Curtain up,* cue Doc to enter.

CUE: Doc puts *skillet in sink.* Cue Marie to enter.

CUE: DOOR SLAM (off stage). Marie and Lola meet off stage on stairs. LOLA: *"Mornin', Honey."*

CUE: STOVE ON. MARIE: "She said he'd be here at *9:30."*

CUE: LIGHT Cue #1—(kitchen down). MARIE: *"O.K. thanks."*

CUE: Sound Cue #1 (airplane sneaks in from distance, passes, and fades out). LOLA: "Little Sheba, come, come back—come back, little Sheba."

CUE: PHONE rings. LOLA: puts coffee ring away, *crosses to sink.*

CUE: Light Cue #2 (kitchen up) ON POSTMAN'S EXIT.

CUE: HORN (2 beeps). MILKMAN: ". . . just takes care of *himself.*"

CUE: LIGHT CUE #2 (kitchen dim). LOLA: cross R. to kitchen door.

CUE: SOUND CUE #2 (Taboo). LOLA turns radio on.

CUE: SOUND SWITCH OFF: MARIE turns RADIO OFF.

CUE: LIGHT CUE #4 (kitchen up). Doc: cross left to kitchen.

CUE: Doc: "I'll never forgive *you.*" *Doc on 2nd step 8 stairs.* FAST CURTAIN—SOUND CUE #3 (Jungle Fantasy in pit). FOOTS TO GLOW. PROP SHIFT.

ACT ONE—Scene II

CUE: SOUND CUE #4 (Ava Maria). LOLA: "I'll be right back." Doc goes to radio—turns it on.

CUE: LIGHT CUE #1 (Living room chandelier on, areas up). LOLA AT SWITCH: ". . . you think I'd be *pooped.*"

CUE: SOUND CUE #5 (SWITCH TO "I've found a New Baby"). LOLA: "Let's get some peppy music." *SHE SWITCHES DIAL.*

CUE: SOUND SWITCH OFF. Doc: "And give away all my secrets?" (Doc AT RADIO: *TURNS DIAL OFF.)*

CUE: SOUND CUE #6 (RHUMBA). LOLA: "Let's have some music." (Doc *TURNS ON RADIO.)*

CUE: SOUND SWITCH OFF. Doc: "That's all forgotten now." (HE TURNS RADIO OFF.)

Cue: SOUND CUE #7, 7A, 7B 7C (Varsity Drag). Lola: "Let's have some music." *(SHE TURNS RADIO ON.)*

Cue: LIGHT CUE #3 (CHANDELIER LIVING ROOM OUT—AREAS DOWN) Lola: "I steamed it open and sealed it back." Turk *AT LIVING ROOM LIGHT SWITCH.*

Cue: LIGHT CUE #4 (BEDROOM LIGHT OUT) after Marie leaves her room. Turk: "Biology? Hot dog."

Cue: CUE—Lola UP STAIRS: Doc: Looks at bottle twice and as he starts the *third look CUE.*

Cue: LIGHT CUE #5—Doc TURNS OUT THE KITCHEN LIGHTS. (Kitchen chandelier out. Areas out.) CUE: *DOC AT SWITCH.*

Cue: LIGHT CUE #6 (UP STAGE AREAS DOWN.) Turk: "Let's get to work." *THEY SIT COUCH.*

Cue: SOUND CUE #9—(START OTHER RECORD.) Turk: "Not tonight Turk."

Cue: LIGHT CUE ⁻#7 (Areas down.) THEY START TO DANCE. *TURK TURNS OFF LAMP.*

Cue: CURTAIN: Lola: "Little Sheba . . . come back . . . come back . . . Little Sheba. Come *back."*

When Curtain is down—house up—Orchestra start.

INTERMISSION

ACT TWO, Scene I

Cue: House to half—Orchestra stop—House Out—Curtain up.

Cue: TURK'S LAUGH FROM BEDROOM. CUE when Doc crosses from kitchen D.R. living room and picks up Marie's scarf.

Cue: DOC'S ENTRANCE. MRS. COFFMAN exits

and MARIE *waves Turk out from center of platform.*

CUE: CUE LOLA UP STAIRS. DOC: takes coat from closet and *crosses to bottle CUE.*

CUE: MEDIUM FAST CURTAIN SOUND CUE #1 (as curtain starts). LOLA: "It's a beautiful day. There isn't a cloud in *sight.*"

ACT TWO, Scene II

CUE: PHONE RINGS. LOLA: ". . . you two young *lovebirds.*"

CUE: SOUND CUE #2 (tales from Vienna Woods) —CURTAIN—SOUND SHIFT TO PIT (when Curtain is down). LOLA: "Let's have a little music. *LOLA TURNS ON RADIO.*

ACT TWO, Scene III

CUE: LIGHT CUE A. LOLA: sits chair D.R.

CUE: LIGHT CUE #1 (General brightening). DOC: "Good morning, *Honey.*"

CUE: SOUND CUE #3 (airplane). DOC: "Lola, my pretty Lola." *He falls.*

CUE: LIGHT CUE #2 (areas up). LOLA: "Would you please, Mrs. Coffman?"

CUE: (brightening). ED: "They'll sober you up."

CUE: LIGHT CUE #4. LOLA: "Yes . . . yes . . . *Mrs. Coffman.*" (Mrs. Coffman exits.)

CUE: PHONE RING. BRUCE EXIT (2 counts)— then RING.

CUE: CURTAIN. LOLA: "and tell Daddy *hello.*"— then foots UP.

ACT TWO, Scene IV

CUE: SOUND Q #4 (band music at the stadium). MRS. COFFMAN: "All the athletes from the college are supposed to be *there.*"

CUE: MAILMAN ENTERS PORCH, on MRS. COFFMAN'S exit.

CUE: MILKMAN ENTERS on POSTMAN'S exit.

CUE: FADE OUT SOUND—LOLA: "Are you all right, Doc?"

CUE: LIGHT CUE #1—LOLA: "So do I. . . . Have you had your breakfast, Doc?"

CUE: CURTAIN—LOLA: "I'll fix your *eggs*."

CURTAIN CALLS

#1 COMPANY
#2 (stage L. to R.) Ed, Milkman, Bruce
#3 "   "   "   "   Mrs. Coffman, Postman
#4 "   "   "   "   Marie, Turk
#5 "   "   "   "   Doc, Lola
#6 "   "   "   "   Doc alone
#7 "   "   "   "   Lola alone
#8 "   "   "   "   Doc, Lola, joined by COMPANY
Last Curtain down CUE: HOUSE UP
ORCHESTRA START.

COME BACK, LITTLE SHEBA

LIGHT PLOT

Lamp	Type	Hot Spot	Color	Plugged
BALCONY:				
1	Leko	Area 1, 2, 3	29	A7
2	DEAD			
3	Leko	Area 1	120	A10
4	Leko	Area 2	120	A10
5	Leko	Area 3	120	A10
6	Leko	Area 4	120	A11
7	Leko	Area 1, 2, 3	112	A12
8	Leko	Area 5	120	A11
9	Leko	Area 6	120	A11
10	Leko	Area 1	72	A10
11	Leko	Area 2	72	A10
12	Leko	Area 3	72	A10
13	Leko	Area 4	112	A11
14	Leko	Area 4, 5, 6	112	A13
15	Leko	Porch	29	B7
16	Leko	Porch	112	A1
17	Leko	Area 5	112	A11
18	Leko	Area 6	112	A11
1st PIPE:				
1	Leko	Area 1	120	A9
2	Leko	Area 2	120	A9
3	Leko	Area 3	120	A9
4	Leko	Stove	120	A12
5	Fresnel	C. Chair	112	A12
6	Leko	Area 4	120	A8
7	Leko	Area 5	120	A8
8	Leko	Area 6	120	A8
9	Fresnel	R. Chair	112	A12

82

10	Leko	U.C. Kitchen	72	A12
11	Leko	Telephone	112	B4
12	Leko	U.C. Liv. Rm.	112	A13
13	Leko	Area 1	72	A9
14	Leko	Area 2	72	A9
15	Leko	Area 3	72	A9
16	Leko	Telephone	72	B4
17	Fresnel	U.C. Liv. Rm.	112	A13
18	Fresnel	Set U.R.	112	A13
19	Leko	Door R.	72	A13
20	Leko	Area 6	72	A8
21	Leko	Area 5	72	A8
22	Leko	Area 4	72	A8
Tower	1000W			
D.R.	Fresnel	Porch	112	A2
Tower	500W			
D.R.	Fresnel	Porch	112	A2
Pipe	1000W			
R.	Fresnel	Porch	112	A1
Foots	Baby			
	Fresnel	Porch	112	A1
Tower	1000W			
D.L.	Projector	Door D.L.	Dbl 29	B2
Tower	500W			
D.L.	Fresnel	Clothes Line	112	A3
Tower	500W			
D.L.	Fresnel	Door D.L.	112	A3
Stand	750W			
L.	Leko	Kit. Window	112	A3
Pipe	1000W			
L.	Projector	Kit. Window	112	A1
Tower	750W			
D.R.	Leko	Porch	Dbl 29	B7
Pipe	750W			
R.	Leko	Porch	Dbl 29	B7
Pipe	1000W			
L.	Projector	Kit. Window	Dbl 29	B8
Pipe	500W			
R.	Fresnel	Foliage	112	A2

Stand Bedr'm	Fresnel	Bed	72	B1
Stand Bedr'm	Fresnel	Bed	120	B1
Pipe L.	Leko	Hall	120	B5
Stair Beam	Baby Fresnel	Hall	120	B5

3 Sections of 300W X-Rays on Pipe R.:

			72	B12
			120	B13
			31	B14

2 Sections of 300W X-Rays on Pipe L.:

			72	B9
			120	B10
			31	B11

Living room floor lamp	A4
Living room table lamp	A5
Living room chandelier	A6
Kitchen chandelier	B3
Stove hotplate	B6

CONTROL:

2—14 Plate 3000W master switchboards
1—12 Plate 500W preset board. (All lamps on switches
 A-12 and 13 plugged on presets. 1st PIPE #18
PRESET AT PT5 EXCEPT IN SCENE 2-3)

LIGHT CUES

ACT ONE, Scene I

Setup:

A-Board:	B-Board:
1—Full	1—pt 7
2—Full	4—pt 5
3—Full	5—pt 8
8—pt 2	9—pt 3
9—pt 2½	10—pt 3
10—pt 4	12—Full

    11—pt 3   13—Full
    12—pt 3
    13—pt 3
Cue #1
A-12 down to pt 5
Cue #2
A-1w up to pt 3
Cue #3
A-12 down to pt 5
Cue #4
A-12 up to pt 3

ACT ONE, Scene II

Setup:

A-Board:		B-Board:
4—ON		1—pt 3
		(See note on Cue #2)
5—ON		2—pt 5
7—pt 10 (After Curtain)		3—ON
8—pt 6		4—pt 7½
9—pt 3		7—FULL
10—pt 3		8—FULL
11—pt 4		10—pt 8
12—pt 4		11—pt 3
13—pt 4		13—pt 5
		14—pt 3

Cue #1
A-6—ON
A-8—pt 2
A-11—pt 3
Cue #2
B-1—ON at pt 3 (This cue used only if desired—
   otherwise Bedroom is on at opening.)
Cue #3
A-6—OUT
A-8—pt 4
A-11—pt 5
A-13—pt 6

Cue #4
B-1—OUT
Cue #5
Fade out B-4 on Warning to this cue
B-3—OUT
A-9—OUT
A-10—OUT
A-12—OUT
Cue #6
B-2—down to pt 7, B-7 and 8 down to pt 3 on Warning this cue.
A-13—Fade OUT
Cue #7
A-4—OUT
A-7—pt 8
A-11—pt 8

ACT TWO, Scene I

Setup:

A-Board:	B-Board:
1—FULL	1—pt 5
2—FULL	4—pt 3
3—FULL	5—pt 8½
8—pt 2	9—FULL
9—pt 4	10—FULL
10—pt 3	12—FULL
11—pt 4	13—FULL
12—pt 3	
13—pt 4	

ACT TWO, Scene II

Setup:

A-Board:	B-Board:
4—ON	1—pt 7
6—ON	2—pt 6
8—pt 4	3—ON
9—pt 4	4—pt 3
10—pt 3	5—pt 8

11—pt 4   7—pt 1
12—OUT   8—pt 1
13—pt 4   10—pt 6
                             11—pt 2
                             13—pt 6
                             14—pt 1

ACT TWO, Scene III

A-Board: B-Board:
  1—pt 8   4 - pt 9½ (Mark)
  2—pt 9½   9—pt 8
  3—pt 8   10—pt 8
  8—pt 7   11—pt 8
  9—pt 7   12—pt 5
  10—pt 8   13—pt 5
  11—pt 8   14—pt 5
  12—OUT
  13—pt 8
(Presets 8, 9, 10, 11, 12 at Pt 6)

(NOTE: Cues that follow in this scene have switches
    listed in order which moves are made)

Cue #A
A-10—pt 7
A-11—pt 7
A-8—pt 6
A-9—pt 6
A-13—pt 5
B-4—pt 9
Cue #1
B- 9—pt 7½   A-10—pt 6
B-10—pt 5½   A-11—pt 6
B-12—pt 5
B-13—pt 3
Cue #2
B- 1—pt 8   A- 1—pt 5 ⎫ Move halfway—move
B- 9—pt 5½   A- 2—pt 5 ⎬ others—then return
B-10—pt 5½   A- 3—pt 5 ⎭ and finish

B-12—pt 2½   A- 9—pt 4½
B-13—pt 2½   A-10—pt 4½
                    A-12—pt 7
                    B- 4—pt 7½

Cue #3
A- 8—pt 5   B- 6—ON
A-11—pt 5   B- 9—pt 5
A-13—pt 3   B-10—pt 5
                    B-12—pt 2
                    B-13—pt 2

Cue #4
B- 9—4½   A-13—pt 1
B-10—4½
B-12—1½
B-13—1½

ACT TWO, Scene IV

Setup:

A-Board:	B-Board:
1—FULL	1—pt 7
2—FULL	4—pt 5
3—FULL	5—pt 8
8—pt 2	9—pt 3
9—pt 2½	10—pt 3
10—pt 5	12—FULL
11—pt 4	13—FULL
12—pt 4	
13—pt 4	

Cue #1
A- 9—pt 1½
A-10—pt 4
A-12—pt 3
A- 8—pt 3
A-11—pt 5

COME BACK, LITTLE SHEBA

WORKING PROPERTY PLOT

Easy Chair D.R.
On it:
Marie's pocketbook containing chiffon scarf, lipstick, etc.

Side Table by Chair
On it:
Small table radio
Newspaper from small Midwestern town

Old-fashioned standing floor lamp by chair

Newspapers and magazines scattered on floor D.R. by chair and table

Umbrella stand with umbrellas upstage of front R.

Victorian what-not against wall U.R.C.
On its shelves:
Small silver picture frame (Lola polishes in I-2)
Numerous books, statuary, etc., to dress

Small cabinet R. of staircase
On it:
Bronze eagle with old sweater draped over wing
Box of candy
In it:
Tablecloth folded neatly (used in II-1)

On bannister of staircase:
Old house-dress for dressing

Davenport (4½' long) D.R.C.
On it:
Old house dress at R. end
Magazines and papers on couch and on floor by it

Narrow wing table back of davenport
On it:
Small framed picture of Lola as a girl (L. end)
Antique lamp (C.)
Silver cigarette box, antique (R.C.)
Bowl of grapes, practical (R.)
Magazines and newspapers to clutter up

Small console table-desk L. (Back to stove)
On it:
Small brass letter-rack containing envelopes
Small celluloid toy duck
Papers and magazines to clutter up

End table L. of couch
On it:
Bowl of chocolate candy D.S. end
Deck of playing cards C.
Magazine and newspapers covering these

Kitchen table D.L.C.
On it:
Oilcloth cover
Dishpan containing dirty dishes, pot, dish-rag
Cup and saucer half full of coffee (R.)
Butcher knife (R.)
Dirty glass (L.)
Asbestos mat for coffee pot (D.L.)
Set around it:
3 kitchen chairs

Stove—gas-burner type with electric hotplate hidden in L.C.
On it:
Kettle with hot water D.L. burner
Coffee pot D.R. burner

Dirty frying pan U.L. burner
Salt and pepper shakers on oven top R.
Box of kitchen matches on oven top R.
Cloth pot-holder R.
Cup for burnt matches R.
Telephone scratch pad and pencil R.
Telephone (dial) on shelf fastened to U.S. end stove
    with bell box
In it:
Drawer L.—clean frying pan and fork for Act II,
    Scene 4
Oven—pot and lid for Act II, Scene 2

Hot water tank against wall U.C.
On it:
Checked dish-towel

In Closet U.L.:
Trench coat (Doc) L.
House-dress (Lola) C.
Clean dish-towel R.
2 brooms with dust-cloth on top of handle of one R.
Black shoes (Lola) floor C.
Dustpan floor C.

Old wooden ice-box against side wall U.L.
On top of it:
3 cups and saucers L.
1 small plate and knife R.
Box of soap powder and old paper bags
Litter to dress
In it:
R. compartment:
1 orange
1 can of condensed milk
1 small piece of angel-food cake on plate with knife
1 can of pineapple juice
1 box of eggs (on bottom shelf for dressing only)
L. compartment:
Bottle of water with screw top

Can of pineapple juice
Quart bottle of buttermilk ½ full

Sink against wall L.—practical running water
On drainboard:
Cup and saucer U.L.
Coffee-ring in paper bag D.L.
2 dinner plates D.R.
Wire drain rack containing dirty dishes and cups C.
Dirty dish-rag on D.R. corner of sink
Clean dish-rag hidden in U.R. corner of sink (For Act
    I, Scene 2)
Bar of soap in dish above faucets.

On window ledge above sink:
Alarm clock L.
Old dog's feeding pan R.

Dirty curtains in removeable valance over kitchen win-
    dow.

*Wooden kitchen-cabinet with 4 open shelves, drawers
    and cupboards against wall D.L.*
On top shelf L. to R.:
Box of soda (open, with sugar in it)
3 cans of dog food
1 box of brillo
3 boxes of soap powder
Quart bottle of whiskey, unopened

On 2nd shelf L. to R.:
4 paper bags
1 small can
1 paper bag containing bulk food
2 cups

On 3rd shelf L. to R.:
2 saucers
Sugar bowl
Glass salt and pepper shakers
4 cups stacked messily

On 4th shelf L. to R.:
Cup and saucer
4 water glasses
3 old-fashioned glasses
3 fruit-juice glasses
1 beer-can opener
2 dinner plates leaning against back
3 dinner plates messily stacked

In cupboard, top shelf:
Assorted boxes of breakfast foods, etc., to dress, leaving space for dinner plate to be put in by Lola.

In cupboard, bottom shelf:
Various sized boxes for dressing.

In drawer L.:
Assorted kitchenware spoons, knives and forks
Clean dish-cloth to be used in Act I, Scene 2
Extra beer-can opener

In drawer R.:
Paper bag sticking out messily

Off R.:
Mailman's bag containing assorted letters and papers
Bundle of letters strapped together
Six loose letters
Mailman's whistle
Telegram in envelope lightly sealed at tip of flap
Western Union delivery signature form
Pencil for Western Union delivery boy
Large sketch pad with drawing of Turk started
Drawing pencil

Off Upstage (Marie's room)

Dressing table
On it:
2 school books
Duplicate telegram in sealed envelope
Knick-knacks for dressing

2 straight-backed chairs
Bed with bed-clothes messed up
2 suitcases (for Act II, Scene 3)

Off L.:
Milkman's carrying rack with full milk-bottles
Carton of cottage cheese (not practical)
½ pint of cream (not practical)
Quart of buttermilk
Milk customer's check list
Bill pad
Pound of butter in box (not practical—for Act II,
    Scene 4)

Clothes-line rigged to run outside kitchen window
Assorted children's clothes hanging on line to be pulled
    into sight.
Children's clothes loose (Mrs. Coffman carries on
    stage)

Off U.C.—by stair platform:
Door-slam

ACT ONE, Scene II

Put slip-cover on living-room couch
Strike all newspapers, magazines, sweaters, house-
    dresses, candy-box, etc., in living room *BUT
    LEAVE MIDWESTERN PAPER ON SIDE
    TABLE BY CHAIR D.R.*
Set new standing lamp and table lamp.
Set new curtains and valance on kitchen window. Set
    drainboard skirt. Strike old curtains.
Set row of cannisters on second shelf of kitchen
    cabinet.
Hang all cups on hooks below third shelf of kitchen
    cabinet
Strike all paper bags in cabinet
Dress all shelves neatly
Set clean dish-rag on soap dish, strike dirty dish-rag.

Set new linoleum drain-board and drain-board backing.

Strike old drain-board, drain-board backing, draining rack with dirty dishes, paper bags, dish-pan in sink.

Set new draining-rack with clean dishes.

Strike all trash from top of ice-box, leaving 3 cups and saucers.

Strike all props on kitchen table.

Put pot of beans and spoon on stove.

Move clothes on clothes-line to out of sight-lines.

Off L.:
Jar of silver-polish and rag.

ACT TWO, Scene I

Strike school books from couch.

Strike silver-polish and rag on table D.R.

Move silver picture-frame from table D.R. to what-not cabinet.

Move Lola's picture from what-not cabinet to L. end table behind couch.

Strike cards on floor and deck of cards to in silver box.

Strike candy on end table.

Set Doc's hat on lamp D.R.

Set Marie's scarf on back of chair D.R.

Set 2 glasses of tomato juice in ice-box.

Set clean towel on water heater.

Set on kitchen table:
> 2 cups, saucers and spoons
> Plate with 3 sweet rolls
> 2 empty juice glasses
> Table-cloth

Strike dirty dishes on sink and drainboard

Set glass and spoon on drainboard.

Set dishpan containing 4 large and 4 small plates Haviland china in the sink.

ACT TWO, Scene II

Strike scarf from chair D.R.

Strike bowl of grapes and silver box from console table.

Strike props on kitchen table and tablecloth.

Set vase of lilacs on U. stage shelves.

Set vase of lilacs on dining table.

Set single bloom of lilac beside vase for Marie's hair.

Set two silver candlesticks with tall candles on table.

Set book of paper matches on table.

Set silver for four beside plates on dining table.

Set on kitchen table: 4 cups and saucers in a row, 3 platters, gravy boat and half-full bottle of milk.

Set covered pot on stove.

ACT TWO, Scene III

Strike table setting, leaving only:
    2 small plates
    2 napkins
    Vase of flowers
    Candlsticks

Replace tall candles with short ones.

Move newspaper from table D.R. to console table.

Strike all props on kitchen table.

Strike chair R. of kitchen table.

Set chair L. of kitchen table to against kitchen cabinet.

Set coffee pot on R. burner of stove.

Set on drainboard:
    2 clean cups
    2 glasses
    1 whiskey glass

Off L.:

Hatchet (Prop man hand it to Doc).

Whiskey bottle full of coke and water to be opened and drunk.

Personal:

Engagement ring (Marie).

ACT TWO, Scene IV

Strike glass and coffee cup D.R.
Strike Doc's hat from D.R. to prop table off R.
Strike whiskey bottle from console table.
Strike tablecloth, plates, flowers, candlesticks, etc.
Strike lilacs on U. stage shelves.
Set dining table to behind couch.
Set table lamp on table.
Set Lola's picture on table.
Strike Doc's coat from kitchen to Doc's dressing room.
Set bacon in ice-box (keep on ice 'til now).
Set frying pan on stove D.L. burner.
Set cooking fork on stove.
Set kitchen chairs to Act I, Scene 1 posits (including
    one struck Act II, Scene 3).
Set coffee pot on stove.
Hand dust rag to Lola.

Off R.:
Suitcase for Doc.

Off L.:
Magazine "Strength and Health."

COME BACK, LITTLE SHEBA

COSTUME PLOT

Lola:

ACT ONE, Scene I

Slip
Green bathrobe
Bedroom slippers
Brown house-dress with green flowers
Black suede pumps

ACT ONE, Scene II

Blue checked house dress
Black slippers
Pink wool sweater

ACT TWO, Scene II

Black and white flower print silk dress—chiffon jacket

ACT TWO, Scene III

Same as Act Two, Scene II, plus pink sweater

ACT TWO, Scene IV

Green checked house dress

Marie:

ACT ONE, Scene I

Blue negligee
Blue bedroom slippers
Blue petticoat
Orange sweater
Grey skirt
Tan shoes

Tan ankle socks
Orange hair-band

ACT ONE, Scene II

Chartreuse blouse
Grey skirt
Brown shoes and socks

ACT TWO, Scene I

Blue dungarees
White shirt
Black belt
Blue shoes
Red hair-band

ACT TWO, Scene II

Green crepe dress
Yellow chiffon band in hair
Yellow shoes

ACT TWO, Scene III

Same as Act Two, Scene II, plus:
Tan summer coat
Small tan handbag

Doc:

2 street suits (changes suit for Act Two, Scene IV)
White shirt
Black shoes
Grey hat
Trench coat (prop)

Turk:

ACT ONE, Scene I

Blue dungarees
White T-shirt
Brown shoes

ACT ONE, Scene II and ACT TWO, Scene I

Grey pants
Leather and wool team jacket
White shirt

Brown shoes

MAILMAN:

Blue mailman's uniform, cap, blue shirt, black shoes

MILKMAN:

White milkman's coveralls, black shoes

MESSENGER:

Western Union jacket and cap
Blue dungarees
Brown shoes

BRUCE:

Grey suit, grey hat, white shirt, black shoes

ED:

Tan jacket, blue trousers, white shirt, black shoes
Tie and blue jacket for Act Two, Scene IV

ELMO:

Blue suit, white shirt, black shoes.

COME BACK, LITTLE SHEBA

SOUND PLOT

EQUIPMENT:

Turntable unit containing two turntables and two pre-amplifiers.

Two master amplifiers (one for emergency use).

Speakers as follows:

1 12″ speaker hung U.C. (airplane effect).

1 12″ speaker on floor off U.L. (band effect).

1 6″ speaker in radio on stage

1 12″ speaker hidden on porch R. as booster to radio speaker.

2 speakers hung in auditorium for scene shift music.

Microphone in basement for musicians.

Cable to connect all above.

SOUND CUES

NOTE: Levels are not indicated as they vary with the house:

ACT ONE, Scene I

Cue #1: Airplane flying over (hanging speaker).

Cue #2: Jungle fantasy and voice (radio speakers).

Cue #3: Jungle fantasy (scene shift) (auditorium speakers).

ACT ONE, Scene II

Cue #4: Ave Maria (radio speakers).

Cue #5: I Found a New Baby (radio speakers).

Cue #6: Bolero Song (Rhumba) (radio speakers)

Cue #7: Varsity Drag, Summertime, You Were Meant for Me (radio speakers).

Cue #8: The Very Thought of You (radio speakers).

ACT TWO, Scene I

Cue #1: The Way You Look Tonight (auditorium speakers).

ACT TWO, Scene II

Cue #2: Tales of the Vienna Woods (radio speakers, then auditorium).

ACT TWO, Scene III

Cue #3: Airplane flying over (hanging speaker).

ACT TWO, Scene IV

Cue #4: Band music (speaker off U.L.).

The above songs are performed through the courtesy of their respective lyricists, composers and publishers: "You Were Meant for Me" by Arthur Freed and Nacio Herb Brown. Published by Robbins Music Corp. "Snowfall" by Claude Thornhill. Recorded by Claude Thornhill and his Orchestra. Published by Mutual Music Society, Inc. "Adversidad" by Gonzalo Curiel. Published by Southern Music Publishing Co., Inc. "The Very Thought of You" by Ray Noble. Published by M. Witmark & Sons. "Jungle Fantasy" by Esy Morales. Published by Duchess Music Co. "I've Found a New Baby" by Jack Palmer and Spencer Williams. Published by Pickwick Music Co. "The Way You Look Tonight" by Dorothy Fields and Jerome Kern. "The Varsity Drag" by Buddy DeSylva, Nacio Herb Brown and Ray Henderson. "Where or When" by Richard Rodgers and Lorenz Hart. "Summertime" by Ira and George Gershwin. Published by Chappel and Co.

MUSIC NOTE

Samuel French cannot authorize, in amateur or stock productions of this play, use of the musical numbers referred to in this copy. We would suggest that groups producing the play substitute public domain music.

SOUND EFFECT RECORDS

Samuel French can supply the following sound effect
records used in connection with this play.

#1-2 Come Back, Little Sheba $3.80 postpaid
#3 4 Come Back, Little Sheba $3.80 postpaid
#5-6 Come Back, Little Sheba $3.80 postpaid
#7-8 Come Back, Little Sheba $2.50 postpaid

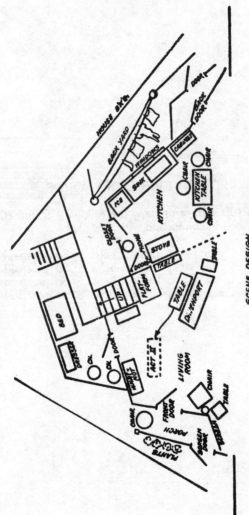

SCENE DESIGN

"COME BACK LITTLE SHEBA"